# ANOTHER
# WORD FOR
# MURDER

## MARC D. HASBROUCK

iUniverse®

# ANOTHER WORD FOR MURDER

*iUniverse books may be ordered through booksellers or by contacting:*

*iUniverse*
*1663 Liberty Drive*
*Bloomington, IN 47403*
*www.iuniverse.com*
*844-349-9409*

*Because of the dynamic nature of the Internet, any web addresses or links contained in this book may have changed since publication and may no longer be valid. The views expressed in this work are solely those of the author and do not necessarily reflect the views of the publisher, and the publisher hereby disclaims any responsibility for them.*

*Any people depicted in stock imagery provided by Getty Images are models, and such images are being used for illustrative purposes only.*
*Certain stock imagery © Getty Images.*

*ISBN: 978-1-6632-5509-9 (sc)*
*ISBN: 978-1-6632-5510-5 (e)*

*Library of Congress Control Number: 2023914237*

*Print information available on the last page.*

*iUniverse rev. date: 08/07/2023*

I Dedicate This Book To My Two Fathers

Ladislaw Fried
*My Birth Father*
(1911 – 1984)
Bronze Star Recipient
World War II

Carlton Joseph Hasbrouck
*My Stepfather*
(1911 – 1986)
Purple Heart Recipient
World War II

# A Short Note From The Author

I just can't leave well enough alone. Or, to put it more succinctly, I can't leave my characters. Period. After creating the mystery writer Devon Stone and his new friends Billy Bennett, Veronica Barron, and Peyton Chase in *Murder On The Street Of Years*, I enjoyed being with them so much that I brought them back for an encore in *Remember You Must Die*. I thought that was it and I had finally said goodbye to these beloved, friendly, brave, loveable, sometimes-sarcastic folks. Well, think again. Not so easy. And not so fast, Hasbrouck! They all kept "speaking" to me from deep within my imagination. Late at night. When I was trying to go to sleep. I heard them loud and clear. They had at least one more story to tell. One more adventure and another mystery to unravel. Of course, Devon Stone's unfailing memory, thanks to hyperthymesia, will continue to rattle both friend and foe. Is it a blessing or a curse?

That being said, I started doing a bit more research and came up with *Another Word For Murder*. This book takes place two years following the action in *Remember You Must Die*, but it is not a sequel, per se. You need not to have read either of the prior two Devon Stone thrillers, although a few fine threads from those first two books are briefly mentioned and interwoven here.

In *Murder On The Street Of Years* my readers learned something about World War II that perhaps they didn't know.

In *Remember You Must Die* my readers discovered yet another little-known fact from World War II and also learned about a deadly section of New York City dating back to the late 1800s and into the early 1900s.

*Remember You Must Die* dealt with coincidences (several of them), happenstance, and being in the wrong place at the wrong time. I read somewhere that coincidences are fine in real life, but in fiction they're just bad writing. Obviously I disagree. I find them utterly fascinating so, needless to say, I had to go back to a theme involving coincidences. Deadly coincidences.

While reading *Another Word For Murder* you will learn a bit about Hong Kong following World War II. Beautiful, exotic, mysterious, and surprisingly dangerous Hong Kong.

With multiple storylines converging in unexpected ways, I ask the same questions in *this* book that I asked in *Murder On The Street Of Years*:

Can murder ever be justified? Can someone actually get away with murder?

Perhaps.

Please bear in mind that I have taken a few liberties with logic and reality. This is a thriller after all, so what else would you expect?

So now, let the action begin!

# PART ONE

---

# DARK FORCES;
# EVIL FORCES

*"If no one knows who you are, you can be whoever you want."*
Fredrik Backman – *The Winners*

# Prologue

*November 5, 1955 – London, England*
*Bonfire Night*

After fits and starts, Devon Stone sat at his desk; once again typing the beginning of chapter ten in his new murder mystery. It had taken him months to get even this far. He had written, rewritten, stopped, started, thrown away and restarted again several times. His creative juices had stalled, and it distressed him. His previous books, all of them best sellers, had come easily and he had played his typewriter like a Stradivarius. Not so now. He wasn't even totally satisfied yet with his working title of *Dressed to Kill.* Having enjoyed the company of a very dapper detective in New York City when he was last there, he is turning the very real, the very congenial Lieutenant James Lafferty into a fictitious central character who gets introduced in this chapter. He chuckled to himself while he wrote, as a small cloud of smoke with the distinct aroma of cannabis swirled around his head.

It hadn't gotten dark yet, but already he heard the sounds of firecrackers being set off up and down his normally quiet street. Londoners take Bonfire Night very seriously. He glanced at his watch as he heard his front doorbell ring.

3

"Blast," he muttered. "Broke my train of thought. Not that I was even on the right track, at that."

It was slightly past cocktail hour and he figured he'd fix himself a nice gin and tonic after answering the door.

A handsome, well-dressed young man, looking to be around his mid to late twenties, smiled as Devon opened the door.

"Good evening, Mr. Stone," he said, tipping his hat, as he handed a small package to the author.

Devon stepped back for a moment. A flashback to another package, albeit left on his doorstep, two years earlier. He glanced at it. No ticking sounds. No *Memento Mori* scribbled across the surface of the wrapping.

"This is from solicitor Blackstone's office, sir. I was asked to deliver this to you and requested that you sign for its receipt."

The young man handed the package to Devon, along with a clipboard and a pen.

Devon hesitated for a brief moment, and then signed the attached form.

"It's an honor to meet you, Mr. Stone," said the young man with a huge smile. "I'm Jesse Thorndike and I've read all of your books, sir. Actually, even more than once or twice."

"I'm flattered, Jesse Thorndike," Devon responded with an even larger smile. "I have no idea who this Mr. Blackstone is, but I'm sure I'm about to find out."

"Yes, sir," Jesse Thorndike said, tipping his hat once again and nodding as he turned to go back down the steps. "Sounds like a war zone out here already, doesn't it? Enjoy the holiday, Mr. Stone."

After closing his front door, Devon shook the package. No sound. Nothing rattling. No ticking bomb seemed to be waiting within.

Devon Stone poured himself a healthy-sized gin and tonic at his bar and carried the package under his arm as he climbed the stairs back to his office. Standing at his desk, he laid the package down, stared at it for a moment, and sipped his drink. The package, firmly wrapped in brown paper and tied with twine, intrigued him. He took another sip and began to unwrap it. There was a cardboard box under the wrappings and he slowly, cautiously lifted the lid. Inside the box was a handwritten note

4

sitting on top of what looked like a manuscript. Before he read the note, he glanced at the top page...the title page...of the manuscript.

**YOU CAN'T GO IN THERE!** *A Thriller by Samuel Fleck*

Devon Stone knew this man. A friend. A fellow author. And one who had committed suicide six months earlier.

Loud fireworks started exploding outside as Devon Stone suddenly plopped down into his chair. He started reading the note.

"Bloody hell!" he exclaimed as he read.

*My dear friend, Devon,*
*I am dead. And soon you will be as well if...*

# 1

*Six months earlier*

It was five minutes past midnight, and Devon Stone lay naked in his bed, wet with perspiration, and trying to catch his breath.

"Happy birthday, Devon," purred his bedded companion. Also naked, sweaty and breathing heavily. "I hope you just enjoyed your early birthday present."

"Ah, my dear sweet Lydia," answered Devon with a broad smile unseen in the nearly pitch-black bedroom. "Half the fun was unwrapping it."

"You *are* a cunning linguist, Devon. You are the most talented author I know."

"May I assume," questioned Devon, "that you might *not* be referring to my writing abilities?"

Lydia Hyui (pronounced *hew*) giggled.

Devon Stone had just turned forty-nine years of age and began his fiftieth year five minutes earlier when the time turned from P.M. to A.M. Lydia was thirteen years his junior.

Raven-haired and with fair, smooth complexion, Lydia spoke with a lilting accent, a delightful combination of British and Cantonese. Following the end of the Japanese occupation of Hong Kong during

World War Two and the resumption of British sovereignty, the population of that city burgeoned rapidly. Too rapidly for Lydia's taste, so she moved from there to London, her Caucasian mother's hometown. Lydia Hyui was exceptionally smart, having easily completed her university studies years earlier in both ancient history and English literature. She now owned a popular and very successful bookstore in the West End, *The Poisoned Quill*, which sold nothing but crime novels and murder mysteries, both current and long-since out of print editions. That is where she had first met Devon Stone. They hit it off right from the start, there was a spark, and now she's an occasional overnight guest.

Lydia was now lying on her stomach. Close beside her Devon was lying on his back. Their bodies were touching. She reached up with her right hand and gently stroked his smooth, well-defined chest playfully caressing one nipple and then the other. Her hand very softly, very slowly moved further down his lean torso. A finger playfully circled his navel before moving a bit further down, following Devon's happy trail. Devon let out a low guttural moan as her hand reached a very private part.

"My, my *my*," cooed Lydia Hyui as she gently tightened her grip, "I think the birthday boy might be ready for another chapter."

Devon Stone laughed.

In one swift move, they both reversed their positions on the bed and Devon was, indeed, ready for another chapter. Perhaps even an epilogue before daybreak if his stamina held out.

At that precise moment, 7:10 A.M. local time, Jian Hyui (pronounced *hew*) was halfway across Victoria Harbour on the Star Ferry. It was a crisp, practically cloudless morning, with sea gulls swooping and calling over the water as they followed the small green and white vessel. The journey between Hong Kong Island to the south and Kowloon Peninsula to the north was a short one, but it was one that Hyui would soon regret and never forget. Both the main and upper decks were packed with passengers, with standing room only. Hyui stood on the main deck, holding on to a supporting post trying to maintain his balance as the boat gently rolled slightly from side to side. As the ferry approached the Wan Chai pier on Hong Kong Island, passengers eagerly began crowding toward the departure exit, moving Jian Hyui shuffling along with them. Suddenly a sinister-looking man standing close behind him withdrew a small knife from his jacket pocket. A gunshot was heard, followed by loud screams as the passengers instantly scattered. Hyui felt a warm liquid hit the back of his neck. He reached his hand back to touch it. When he brought it back around, he recoiled in horror. His hand was covered with blood. It was not his. He turned around, and then looked down at a fallen man practically at his feet. Although part of the man's head was now missing, with blood oozing onto the deck of the ferry, Jian Hyui recognized the man, and his heart started racing. He stared in disbelief.

"*Ngong gau*," he hissed through his taught lips. It was a Cantonese pejorative similar to *asshole*.

The dead man lying at Jian Hyui's feet still loosely clutched a knife. Hyui was more confused than frightened. *What was he about to do to me?* Hyui thought. *Considering that the blood splattered onto the back of my neck, this man must have been shot from behind.*

But by whom? And why?

The now shocked passengers lunged for the exit gangplank as soon as the ferry had finally docked, pushing frantically past the stunned Jian Hyui, knocking him off-balance. With the uncertainty of what was really happening came fear. That fear turned into anxiety, which, then turned into panic. Passengers on the top deck obviously had not seen what was going on but having heard the gunshot and the subsequent shouts and screams from the lower deck had created a panic amongst them as well. They flowed down the stairs and onto the main deck like a raging uncontrolled waterfall. Some were shouting, some of the women were crying, although they didn't know why, and some were screaming. They all ran, pushing and shoving. It was confusion and chaos. Police on the pier had heard the shot and were rushing toward the ferry, fighting against the horrified stampede of humanity as it departed the boat and ran off down the pier toward dry land. Hyui, trying to maintain his balance as the boat rocked and swayed in the waters, slowly looked up from the dead body and caught sight of a tall, handsome Caucasian man toward the back of the ferry. Making eye contact, the man smiled at Hyui, gave him a slight, friendly salute tipping a couple fingers toward his forehead and then nodded his head. The remaining fleeing passengers had paid no attention to him as he casually strolled over to the harbor side of the ferry. He smiled at Hyui once again as he nonchalantly dropped his gun into the water.

Jian Hyui had absolutely no idea who the man was. He had never seen him before.

# 2

Daybreak was just barely beginning to chase the nighttime darkness from the sky. Devon Stone woke up in an empty bed. He inhaled deeply and enjoyed the aroma left behind on the pillow next to his. Lydia Hyui's intoxicating perfume. Guerlain's Véga, with gentle hints of jasmine and ylang-ylang. As a boyish grin crept across his face, he rolled over, inhaled once again and drifted back into a light, peaceful hazy sleep.

Jian Hyui stood stock still in bewilderment. The remaining flow of frightened passengers still rushing past bumped into him, spinning him around in their frantic haste to get off the boat and he nearly fell. Regaining his balance once again, Hyui quickly turned back around again to look for the man. But where was he? The boat was now completely empty. The mysterious Caucasian man just seemed to have disappeared. He must have blended in somehow and slipped right past Hyui unnoticed in the loud frenzied confusion.

Hyui turned around once again and joined the remaining passengers fleeing the ferry. He nearly stumbled as he crossed the gangplank because the small boat was rocking so violently as a result of the rush of people.

Regaining his footing, he turned once again to quickly glance back at the empty ferry before proceeding to run onto Gloucester Road, blending in with the rest of the frightened crowd.

The men who had been lassoing the mooring lines to the dock were bewildered by the panicky departure of the normally serene, usually slow moving morning rush hour passengers. The few crewmembers on the boat that had thrown the lines had then joined the rapidly departing throng. The pilot of the vessel, stepping from the small navigational bridge, stood in a state of alarm and bewilderment following the screams and shouts of his passengers. He then let out an audible gasp as he saw the body, obviously having bled out, lying on the deck floor a few feet in front of him.

Devon Stone slowly rolled out of bed, yawned, and padded, naked, to his floor-to-ceiling bedroom window. All of the buildings along Carlingford Road in Hampstead were row houses, connected side-by-side, having been built sometime before 1890. His house was in the middle of the block so the only windows in his house were in the front and rear. He thrust open the long heavy drapes and faced nothing but pure, stark white. Another foggy day in London. A pea souper, as the natives call it.

"If you were trying to either impress or shock your neighbors, Devon," chuckled Lydia Hyui as she entered his bedroom door, "you must be disappointed. For what it's worth, *I'm* impressed. Such a beautiful ass."

Lydia crossed the room, diaphanous silk robes flowing, and carrying two cups of steaming Black Tea.

He slowly turned around to brazenly face her, placing his hands on his narrow, firm hips.

"Ooh, well, now!" she exclaimed, looking him up and down. "Now I'm *really* impressed. Pardon a grammatical metaphor, Hemingway, but I *adore* your dangling participle."

With mock modesty, a laughing Devon Stone grabbed an end to one of the draperies, pulling it across himself, covering his nakedness.

Thirty minutes later, bathed and dressed, Lydia Hyui gave Devon a quick peck on the cheek as she headed out of his bedroom door.

"My shop should be opening in twenty minutes and it won't be happening without me, dear boy."

"It's not as though you risk being retrenched should you be tardy," chuckled Devon.

Lydia laughed, shaking her head and rolling her eyes.

"Happy birthday once again," she said "...oh, and look around."

She hurried down the hallway, heels clicking on the hardwood floors, and called back to him as she ran down the stairs. "Don't be a stranger!"

He heard his front door close a second later.

Looking around, he saw a small gift-wrapped package on his nightstand. Unwrapping it, his eyes grew wide.

It was a book. *A Study In Scarlet*, by Arthur Conan Doyle. The book had been written in less than three weeks time when the author was twenty-seven, and it was the very first novel in which Sherlock Holmes and Dr. Watson are introduced to readers. He gently opened the cover of the precious old gift. It was a first edition, in excellent condition, published in 1888. And the author had signed it. Not knowing if a signed copy even existed, Devon Stone had been searching for this for several years. He carefully leafed through the pages, stopping here and there to admire the drawings done by Charles Doyle, the author's father. A tear came to his eye as he pressed the beloved prize to his bare chest. He sighed deeply.

Still naked, he padded down the hall to his office, which was lined, ceiling to floor, with bookshelves, which were mostly filled. He slid his newest prize into a space to the left of several other similarly leather-bound volumes.

"And now, at long last, *this* collection is complete," he said to himself.

Jian Hyui slowed his pace. It was a long walk from the pier, up Gloucester Road, to Percival Street and the Lee Theatre. There were several other pedestrians on the sidewalk moving in both directions, but he kept his gaze down not wanting to make eye contact with anyone. A few rickshaws and the bus that he would normally be taking on this journey passed by, but he wanted to walk. To take his time. To process what had just happened.

He felt now, for sure, that his life must have been in danger. The murdered man on the Star Ferry had threatened him recently, but Hyui had assumed they were simply idle threats, perhaps jealousy-based. But who had killed *him*? And why? He racked his brain as he walked, trying to place the Caucasian man who, obviously, just shot and killed the man in the middle of Victoria Harbour. Even more perplexing was the fact that Hong Kong had a strict ban on the private possession of firearms. Obviously that man had taken a great risk.

Although it was a crisp spring morning, with a gentle breeze off the water, Hyui had perspiration on his brow by the time he reached for the stage door of the theatre. He knew it would be unlocked at this time, and cautiously glanced around before entering. As hoped, apparently he had not been followed. He pulled the door shut behind him and when he turned around he was in total darkness.

He knew where the light switch was located and instinctively reached for it. The lights came on in a flicker and he let out a startled little yelp as he jumped back a couple steps. He was almost face to face with a very disgruntled looking woman, scowling and with clenched fists planted firmly on her hips.

"Nǐ wèishéme chídào?" she asked in Mandarin. *Why are you late?*

# 3

Hong Kong in the early 1950s was chaotic, trying to regain British sovereignty following the Japanese occupation during World War Two. There was also the renewal of the Nationalist-Communist Civil war in Mainland China. Hence, a large influx of mainland refugees fled to the city trying to escape the conflict. Hong Kong's population surged from 600,000 to 2.2 million, with the city struggling to accommodate all of these immigrants. With the unrest in China, businesses began to relocate their assets from Shanghai to Hong Kong initiating an economic and cultural rejuvenation.

However, along with the rich farmers and capitalists flowing into the city, a criminal element arrived as well: influential and dangerous crime gangs, called Sān Hé Huì or, translated, Triad societies, which had existed in Mainland China since around the early 1840s. There were two distinct types of these criminal organizations: loosely organized groups known as *Dark Forces, Evil Forces* and the *Black Societies*, a much more mature level of criminal syndicates. Eventually there were between fifty to sixty separate Triad societies active in Hong Kong and it was estimated that one in every six residents belonged to one. The Triad activities varied from the so-called victimless crimes such as prostitution and gambling to the more violent and predatory crimes such as extortion, robbery, and drug trafficking.

The name Triad comes from their three-sided sacred symbol representing heaven, Earth, and humanity. They also maintain an impenetrable code of secrecy.

On a more positive note, the immigrants fleeing from Shanghai brought their love for a particular type of entertainment as well: the Cantonese Opera. Dating as far back as the 13$^{th}$ century, during the Southern Song dynasty, this theatrical art form grew in popularity throughout the years. Many of the well-known operas performed these days originated during the Ming Dynasty. It is a traditional Chinese art form involving music, singing, martial arts, acrobatics, and acting. Children who are interested in this particular art form start at a very young age and go through very strict, tough training. The stretching exercises that they must endure can cause pain but they must follow their instructions otherwise they will be severely scolded by their teacher or, worse, banished from practicing. Traditionally men performed all of the female roles. Successful Cantonese businessmen in Shanghai had their own opera companies and, with their fan-base moving swiftly to Hong Kong, new opportunities arose. The Chinese government created newspaper platforms, Ta Kung Pao and Chang Cheung Hua Pao, to promote the Cantonese Opera to a new and now widening Hong Kong audience.

Aside from the exploding population then, two growing factions existed within the Hong Kong area: crime and culture.

And Jian Hyui was connected to both.

# 4

Wong Lau-Soeng, known to everyone as simply Lau, didn't wait for Jian Hyui's answer about his tardiness. She turned on her heels and marched stridently with a purpose down the long dark backstage hallway, her loose black Shaolin Arhat robe fluttering with each stride. Hyui followed silently with head bowed, listening to the clicking of her heels, and wondering how he might explain the blood, now dried, on the back of his neck. If she even noticed it.

Lau gave the outward appearance of being a small, beautiful, and demure young woman. She was neither young *nor* demure. Her skin smooth as silk at fifty-seven, and with stark, shiny black hair, cut short, with tight bangs straight across her forehead she looked like a fragile porcelain doll. She was *not* fragile. For that matter, she was lethal.

She was a master in Ving Tsun, a style of close-combat kung fu. While its origins are up for debate, it is widely thought that Shaolin monks first developed this style of the martial arts during the 18th century.

Devon Stone was still naked as he went to answer his telephone.

"Good morning, Stone, hope I haven't awakened you. I know you're not an early riser," said his caller, James Flynn, Devon's London-based publisher.

"Oh, no, that's fine," answered Devon chuckling to himself. "I was up early this morning."

"Yes, well, then," answered Flynn, "I have a bit of disturbing news, I'm sorry to say."

"Oh?" was Devon's response. "I know I'm way behind on my next book, is that why you're calling me at the crack of dawn? To admonish me or to sever our relationship?"

"Don't be ridiculous, my boy. Not that or anything *like* that at all. No, not at all. To get to my point, I know you are friends with Samuel Fleck."

"Yes, I am indeed, James. Sad to say, though, his last few books have been dreadful, haven't they? His writing has been *way* off. And I know his sales suffered as a result. I hesitated to even talk to him about it, but I was concerned. Frankly, it was so horrible that it was embarrassing. Has he jumped ship and gone to a new publisher?"

"Hmm. Yes, well, in a manner of speaking he *did* jump ship. I just found out that he was discovered dead late last night. The authorities are thinking apparent suicide I was told."

Devon Stone was uncharacteristically silent for a moment.

"Wise career move, I'd say," he responded to the news. "Oh, shite, that sounded ghastly. Sorry I even *thought* it, much less *said* it. Forgive me. Poor chap. I didn't realize he had become that despondent."

'That's what has me flummoxed," answered James Flynn. "We met the night before last. He called and asked to meet with me at *your* favorite little pub, The Thorn Bush. He was positively ebullient. Best I've seen him in years. He wouldn't divulge any details, but said he had just finished his latest book and said it was the absolute best book he had ever written. Said it would put him back on track and guaranteed that all his faithful followers would *love* it. He laughed a bit when he said it was a roman à clef and if anyone could figure out the real characters behind his fictional ones, they'd not be thrilled. He hinted that it was licentious and highly indiscreet. And then he ups and does *this* idiotic maneuver."

"That's certainly odd," said Devon Stone shaking his head. "How did he do it? And did he ever send you the manuscript?"

"No, the manuscript was not sent. Now that he's dead, I don't know if and when we might get it. If ever. I haven't a clue where it might be. At his residence, I'm assuming. Regarding his suicide? The authorities wouldn't or *couldn't* tell me much. An investigation is obviously just beginning. The Times, The Guardian, and The Daily Telegraph are all keeping fairly mum about it this morning for some reason. That's why I wanted to contact you before you found out via the retched media. Apparently he was found dead by his housekeeper, sitting in an easy chair in his living room. According to her, he was home alone all evening. Alone the entire day, for that matter. Evidently he must have been reading one of *your* earlier books. It was still on his lap when his body was found. They hinted at drug overdose, but it's still not conclusive. An empty pill bottle was found on the floor at his feet and a nearly empty glass of wine was on a table next to his chair. Nothing further. I knew that occasionally he might take a mild medication for dyspepsia, but I can't imagine that anyone would…or even *could* overdose on something like that. But what do I know, eh? I'm only a publisher."

"I repeat," said Devon, "poor chap. I know his wife died a few years ago when we had that dreadful two-week period of the black, deadly fog killing thousands of Londoners. Does he have any other living survivors? I remember he had a son, didn't he? But he rarely spoke of him."

"You remember *everything*, Devon. Yes, he has a son who's been living somewhere in the Orient since after the war. I think he's been living in Beijing…or maybe Peking. Or was it Hong Kong? I can never remember."

"Well," answered Devon Stone shrugging his shoulders, "Beijing and Peking are the exact same place, just different names, so that must narrow it down to only two places. Unless, of course, you might want to throw out another locale at random. How about Rangoon? That has a nice ring to it. And it's fun to say."

"Don't be a bloody smartass, Stone," responded James Flynn. "And you're absolutely correct. Fleck never spoke of him. In any event, and in whatever city he might be, needless to say, I have no way of contacting him. I never met him. Never communicated with him in any way. I'm assuming that the lad must still be alive. Maybe the authorities might uncover that information from his housekeeper. I've never met *her* either, only spoken with her a few times on the telephone when I've called."

"I am truly saddened to hear this, James, despite my *extremely* callous and inappropriate comment a few moments ago. Fleck and I hadn't communicated in several months. Possibly even a year. He was a better friend to *me* than I was to him. I now regret that."

"Before I ring off, Stone, I *shall* approach the matter of *your* next book to which you alluded at the start of this conversation. Maybe I should say *reproach*. Can you give me any tidbits to whet my appetite?"

"I'm toying with a few ideas, James. Can't honestly and truly say any more. I keep bumping into brick walls with my ideas lately. Frustrating, I realize...for the both of us. Don't worry, I'll come through. Just, please be patient. This news you just hit me with has me depressed now. I wish I could have done something."

"What in blazes *could* you have done, Stone? You had no idea. None of us did. Perhaps I shouldn't have been so harsh with him whenever we spoke over the past few months. Our relationship became very tense and our conversations terse, to say the least. He was disturbed by all the negative reviews and lack of sales. I didn't offer any encouraging words. God knows I could have. I should have."

They ended the call and Devon sat down on the side of his bed, elbows on knees and his head down, thinking about his departed fellow-writer. With his mood boomeranging back and forth from the euphoria of the sensual pleasures earlier in the morning to the startling and depressing news of his friend's suicide.

What neither Devon Stone nor James Flynn knew at the time was that the recently deceased author, Samuel Fleck, had a framed photo of his son, Jeremy, on his desk in his home office. The handsome, well-dressed young man was leaning against a railing, smiling at the camera, with the skyline of Hong Kong in the background reflecting in blue water. He was in the middle of Victoria Harbour and he was riding the Star Ferry.

# 5

Devon Stone laid back soaking in a hot bath, his mind racing with conflicting thoughts. What would prompt his friend, Samuel Fleck, to commit suicide? Why would he be sitting, apparently nonchalantly, reading a book, any book, and then overdose on medication or whatever was in that bottle? If, indeed, whatever was in that bottle was what had killed him. If he had suspected that his newest book had the potential to upset anyone, could that person (or persons) be aware of what was in that book already? But supposedly, according to the housekeeper, Fleck had been home alone all day.

Something just seemed to be off. Something was not quite right about the situation. It sounded like a weird scenario. But Devon thought he'd just let the proper authorities handle it in their way and in their own time. Yes, it was upsetting but it was certainly not his concern. And, yes, it was *very* disturbing but he was not going to get involved in any way. He couldn't and he certainly shouldn't. He had another mystery with which to contend: his own unwritten one. The one with too many brick walls.

He had thought about writing his latest book built around the murders of the Soviet Night Witches following World War Two but then came to the realization that perhaps *that* topic just might open too many doors that were best left closed for the time being.

He had read about and was intrigued by the still unsolved murder of Robert Parrington Jackson back in 1946. At thirty-three, he was the manager of a large cinema house in Bristol and was shot dead in his office during the showing of the film *The Light That Failed.* Two thousand people were in the audience at the time, watching the film, and they had been unaware of the killing. Although robbery had been the suggested motive, the key to the safe remained in the murdered man's pocket and the money in the safe had been untouched. *Intriguing possibilities,* Devon thought. A locked-room murder mystery, not unlike some of his friend Agatha Christie's books.

He had begun with this mysterious situation…and then hit another brick wall. The topic just wasn't his style and he quickly became bored with it.

Lately Devon had simply sat in front of his typewriter slowly drumming his fingers on his desk. Had he hit burnout?

He had had an extremely successful book tour in the United States following the publication of his last book, but that had followed a couple of harrowing experiences involving his own safety.

He had been a stalker of miscreants and a victim himself of near-death situations. He wrote fictional murders, but he didn't relish the idea of being part of actual murder attempts on his life, although he hadn't minded actually killing those who deserved it. Justifiable murders he rationalized. But only a select few people knew of those. Discretion was assured.

Devon Stone finally stepped from his bath, dried off, wrapped a large towel around his waist and plopped back down onto his rumpled bed, which still held the slight hint of jasmine and ylang-ylang.

He knew that he had to dismantle that damn brick wall. Even if it was one brick at a time.

Jian Hyui asked Lau for permission to use the restroom before following her any further into the darkened theatre. Lau sighed loudly but acquiesced and waved him away. The lights to the little dingy backstage bathroom flickered on slowly and he stood looking forlornly into the mirror. *What is happening?* Hyui thought to himself. *How did it come to this?*

He picked up a sponge that rested on the basin, ran it under the water and tried to clean the back of his neck as best he could. He hoped that Lau wouldn't notice or mention the stain now on the back of his shirt collar. There were no towels, so he dried his neck and hands with his handkerchief, quickly putting it back into his pocket.

The feisty woman, still scowling and even more impatient, was waiting for him as he stepped back out of the bathroom.

"Hurry," said Lau, "now go change into the proper attire. We must practice before the others get here. Your movements should take them by surprise. I wish to gauge their reactions. I have high expectations, Hyui."

He hurried to a small dressing room and changed from his street clothes into loose-fitting black pants and a white T-shirt. Again, Lau was right there waiting impatiently for him as he stepped through the door.

Jian Hyui's eyes grew wide with excitement and anticipation as she handed him two long knives. Some called them butterfly knives, others referred to them correctly as Dit Ming Do (Life-taking knives). His mood changed. He smiled. She was training him well.

Lau turned on her heels and marched hastily down the long corridor leading to the rehearsal area as Jian kept pace right behind her. His thoughts, now, were on the knives, one in each hand. His heart rate quickened. His smile widened. For the time being he forgot about the Star ferry, but that early morning incident would soon come back to haunt him, and change him in the most unsuspected way.

# 6

The Cantonese Opera Company was preparing for the debut performance in Hong Kong of their version of *Hua Mulan*, a story that had been well loved for generations with the Chinese. The character of Mulan, a young woman masquerading for years as a man to fight in the army, was considered to be the epitome of the wisdom and goodness of Chinese women.

Jian Hyui followed Lau to the center of the huge stage. The cavernous auditorium was dark and silent. The other performers had not yet arrived for their rehearsals. His heart was beating more rapidly now than when he had been on the deck of the Star Ferry less than two hours before. Starting his training with the Cantonese Opera Company when he was ten years old, now, at the young age of twenty-six, Hyui was one of the popular stars of this opera company. He always played female roles. He had fine features, graceful, fluid moves, and a lilting voice that thrilled his audiences. But this was going to be the most challenging role of his life so far. Here he was, a man, portraying a woman who was pretending to be a man who was the most fearless of warriors amongst an army of men. Lau was about to continue with his lessons in handling those long, deadly knives like an expert. And, of course, without accidently causing any injuries to his fellow performers.

Lau and Hyui faced one another, the long knives in each one of their hands, and began. Soon the sharp sounds of their blades meeting in full swing filled the auditorium.

The rehearsal had gone exceptionally well. The battle scenes in the opera would be extremely well choreographed, graceful ballet moves, with the stunningly sharp blades clanging loudly when swung in pitched one-on-one combat, yet never touching another performer. The effect would be breathtaking. A very satisfied Jian Hyui bowed gently as he completed his lesson.

"Thank you, Sifu Lau," he said, "I am honored that you have taught me so well."

Sifu, pronounced *shifu* in the Cantonese dialect, was the proper way to address a kung-fu master and Lau definitely deserved that distinction. In what had been a highly unusual decision; the opera production company had hired Lau specifically for this particular show to train the performers for the rigorous battle scenes. They wanted the performance to be monumental and unforgettable. But they had no idea what wheels they had set in motion.

Jian Hyui handed the two knives, each as long as his forearm, back to Lau but she waved them off.

"Keep them for now, Hyui," she said sternly. "Practice at home…in the park…up on your rooftop…wherever. The progress you have made this past month is impressive. Much improvement. You learn quickly. Practice. Please, just practice. Your movements will improve even more. Remember, they should be smooth, swift, and quick. Quick as a cat out of a sack. Just try not to kill anyone before our first performance here next month."

Hyui was surprised to see an ever so slight smile appear on the normally stern-faced woman.

"Keep them safe. They have been amongst my vast collection and in my family for generations. Do your job well. If your performance brings gasps from your audience during the opera on opening night, then they will be yours to keep as a reward."

Jian Hyui didn't know how to respond. He was speechless.

Lau was not aware of the demons she may have just unleashed.

Jian Hyui's life was about to change. Dramatically. Dangerously. And deadly.

# 7

While onstage performing, in full costume and exotic makeup, Jian Hyui was a beautiful "woman". Audiences knew, of course, that he was a male but he created such an illusion of graceful beauty that they would have been shocked to see that he was a very ordinary, not particularly handsome young man in reality. He could walk the streets of Hong Kong and Kowloon without being recognized. Almost. He was still extremely confused and tormented about the incident on the Star Ferry earlier in the day. Who was that man who had shot and killed the person directly behind him? For what purpose? He had obviously known who Hyui was, and seemed to be aware that the horrible man behind him was about to do something sinister. The murdered man had been a tormentor for the past year, but Hyui never really took his tormenting seriously. He realized, now, that he has been followed by that mysterious Caucasian, but for what reason and for how long?

He approached the wharf to take the ferry back across the harbor to Kowloon. He was apprehensive and glanced around to see if that mysterious person was following him. Although he carried the long knives that Lau had given to him, he kept them concealed within his garments. The particular boat that he had ridden earlier in the day was cordoned off as a crime scene. When Hyui saw it he momentarily froze. Would someone recognize him from being there when the murder took place and point him out to the authorities?

But the ferry ride back across the harbor was uneventful even if his heart rate had increased.

Despite all the visual opulence, elegance, and grandeur when he appeared onstage, he made the decision to live very modestly and conservatively in a four-story tenement on a street that bordered the very dangerous and notorious *Hak Nam*, the "City of Darkness". This was Kowloon Walled City. With a history dating as far back as the Song dynasty, through the years 906-1279, originally the walled city had been a Chinese military fort. With improvements throughout the centuries, and a formidable defensive wall completed in 1847, it was now an ungoverned and densely populated enclave within Kowloon City itself. It consisted of three hundred and fifty buildings, most of them between ten and fourteen stories high, over eight thousand premises and more than thirty-three thousand residents. The buildings were so tightly packed against one other that the place seemed like one massive, ugly structure. Entering the city meant leaving daylight behind. At street level sunlight could hardly penetrate its narrow, snaking passageways, most of which were just a few feet wide. These alleyways were strewn with refuse thrown out of windows and doors above, attracting scampering rats in every dark shadow. Overhead there were ramshackle dripping corroding plumbing lines surrounded by jumbled dangling bundles of electrical cables. There was a perpetual, acrid smell; some would call it a stench, permeating the area. The combination of pungent aromas from various frying foods blended with the often-overpowering scents from burning incense, garbage and, of course, body odor from the teeming thousands of residents. It had become a cesspool of iniquity. Criminal activity flourished. Five Triad gangs – the King Yee, Sun Yee On, 14K, Wo Shing Wo, and Tai Ho Choi – took up residence. The infamous gangs operated gambling parlors, opium dens and prostitution rings within its shadows, making it so dangerous that police would venture into it only in large groups, if they even ventured into it at all. Despite the many dangers from the underbelly of humanity's flotsam and jetsam, however, countless decent, hardworking families lived within its walls, happy little children played in the narrow, dirty streets, and many small legitimate businesses flourished. Strung along the streets were shops and food stalls, with dog and snake meat often the specialties of the day. A Chinese delicacy se gang, snake soup, was a very popular dish and it contained the meat from as many as five different types of snake. The snakes were killed on site, so the meat was fresh.

Jian Hyui bravely, yet cautiously, frequented the alleyways of the city within a city often and was quite familiar with several of its denizens, criminal and otherwise.

Hyui climbed the steep, narrow, rickety stairs up to his fourth-story flat. Apartments on this floor were numbered in the 300s, with the ground floor apartments starting with G. Buildings in China often avoided utilizing floor numbers with a 4; the number has a similar sound to the word *die* in Cantonese and represented bad luck. The mingling aromas of frying fish and other meats wafting up through the poorly lit stairwell filled his nostrils. The handrails were broken for most of the way up and the stairs were littered with unswept dirt and trash. The hallways leading to each flat were also strewn with dirt, except that the area directly in front of each doorway was spotless. A favorite proverb in China: *Sweep the snow from your own doorstep but don't bother about the ice on your neighbor's roof.* The Chinese were individualists through and through.

Not long after he had moved into his apartment, Jian Hyui had painted his old wooden front door blue, representing the wood element in feng shui. The wood element encourages growth and cultivates kindness along with flexibility.

After a quick sad glance at the doorway directly across the hall from his, he unlocked his door and entered his neatly kept flat, which also adhered to the spiritual concept of feng shui. His flat consisted of a small sparsely furnished living room, a tiny, serviceable kitchen, an even smaller bathroom and his one bedroom with a window that looked out across the street to the foreboding walled city. Despite the cleanliness of his flat, the window was filthy as though it hadn't been washed in years, if ever.

Rushing to his bedroom, he hurriedly changed his clothes. He was not hungry. He would not eat. The sun was down and it was now nearly dark. The germ of an idea had come to him as he rode the ferry back across the harbor following the rehearsal. It frightened him. He had tried to push it from his mind. He fought it, but it relentlessly festered and grew. It was

31

fully manifested by the time the ferry docked at the pier. Something had been merely smoldering inside him. It fully ignited.

*Can I really do this?* Jian thought to himself. *Should I really do this? How can I summon the courage?*

Ten minutes later, now appropriately dressed, Hyui quietly cracked open his front door to peek out; making sure no one was in the hallway that might see him. He then cautiously stepped out into the hallway, locked his door, and quickly went down the creaky stairs. His heart was racing as he went back outside and crossed the street.

To practice.

A sinewy young man, dressed entirely in black, crept back in the shadows along a narrow dank alleyway in Kowloon Walled City. A couple other of his gang members were headed to an opium den a few blocks away and he said he would join them shortly.

After he had gotten some much-needed money.

It would be easy tonight, he thought. He had a butcher's meat cleaver, his weapon of choice, hidden in his jacket, not that he would actually use it on some poor unsuspecting old lady. He would scare her, possibly making her faint, and he could grab whatever cash she might have on her. Something he and his cohorts had done countless times, laughing and giggling in guiltless glee as they then ran away. He turned a corner and saw a potential victim straight ahead, alone, walking away from him. No one else was around. His prey was wearing a long, indigo blue worker-woman's coat and topped by a dǒu lì, a typical conical straw hat. That was odd, but the man didn't give it a second thought because he was an oblivious, over-confident and reckless idiot. He cautiously, stealthily crept up behind his victim.

Closer still.

The person he was pursuing suddenly stopped, perhaps hearing or sensing someone directly behind in the alleyway. The young brigand stepped even closer preparing for an easy robbery.

He pulled the meat cleaver from his jacket just as the person in front of him swiveled around so fast he could hardly see the movement. The straw hat went flying off. The attacker gasped.

This was *not* what he was expecting at all.

"Ni hao, Ngong gau," said the intended victim with a smile, *Hello, asshole.*

The attacker's hand holding the meat cleaver was swiftly and cleanly lopped from his forearm and it bounced, blood spewing from its wrist, onto the dirty, urine-smelling pavement along with the cleaver. Before he had the chance to even scream in pain, his head was severed from his neck just as quickly by a second blade, landing beside his hand. The movements had been smooth, swift, and quick. Quick as a cat out of a sack.

The intended victim who had now become the attacker turned and walked trembling but nonchalantly back down the alleyway, disappearing into the darkness. A rat, then followed by another, scampered out from the shadows and began to sniff the severed head.

With his heart pounding so hard he thought that it would surely burst through his chest, and wondering where the hell he had ever gotten the courage, Jian Hyui had never felt this nervous or as this good in his entire life.

He hurried back to his flat, silently rushing up the stairs and quietly closed his front door. His heart was still racing and his muscles were sore following his strenuous day and evening of swordplay. He was still not hungry. Before he went to bed he opened the small jar of Tiger Balm he kept in his medicine cabinet and smeared the pungent liniment on his arms and shoulders. The instant tingling warmth felt wonderful. He always found the combined aromas of camphor, mint, clove, and menthol soothing.

Staring at his reflection in the mirror he saw a different man than he had seen earlier in the day.

*What have I done?* Hyui thought to himself. *Who am I now? What am I now?*

He climbed into bed, inhaled the scents from the balm, and waited for his nightmares to begin.

# 8

We all have our opinions about death and how we mourn. Or not. Devon Stone considered himself neither an agnostic nor an atheist. He just never gave religion of any kind too much thought. His father had been an atheist for most of his life, but had never made a big deal out of it. His mother had studied dozens of worldwide religions but practiced none of them. As far as she was concerned, they were all pure but intriguing mythology, including Christianity. Actually, the god with whom Devon most closely aligned was Dionysus. He often joked that he hadn't discovered if there even was a god of gin yet, but he praised whichever or whomever the god was who created Gordon's. He acknowledged him (or her) almost on a daily basis.

The week following the unsettling news about his friend's suicide, he received a hand delivered invitation to a memorial service in Samuel Fleck's honor. No formal funeral of any kind, which pleased Devon, just this service to be held at the home of the deceased. Hosted by Jeremy Fleck, son of the deceased. The service was to take place one week from the arrival of the invitation. Devon didn't care for events such as this but he felt compelled to attend. He was certain he would see not only their respective publisher, but also other fellow-writers who knew Fleck.

He took a long sip from his drink, pulled himself up to his typewriter, and tried once again to break down that brick wall. One word at a time. One sentence at a time. One brick at a time.

It had been more years than Devon Stone would like to admit, but he hadn't been to Samuel Fleck's residence in a long time. Fleck's home rivaled Devon's in opulence but for different reasons and in much different ways. Fleck lived in the affluent enclave Chelsea, in West London. His décor was far more old-world, partially wood-paneled, mostly pastel-toned, over-stuffed, and ostentatious, some might even call it flamboyant. Whether it might have been the design sense of his late wife or of Fleck himself, the home simply seemed to scream "old lady". On the other hand, the décor of Devon's home, in the equally posh section of Hampstead, was far more contemporary, masculine, earth-toned, simple, clean and refined, albeit equally as extremely expensive.

Leaving his car at home and electing to take a taxicab instead, Devon took a deep breath as the car pulled up to Fleck's house on Shawfield Street. He didn't know what to expect, but he was certain of one thing: it wasn't going to be a fun evening.

What he *really* hadn't expected, however, was that it was going to be an enlightening, albeit disturbing and perplexing evening.

Several other cabs pulled up in front of the house as Devon climbed the stairs toward the front door. He didn't have to reach for the doorbell because the door opened as he approached. A manservant of some sort stood there in formal attire and nodded as Devon Stone entered.

"Good evening, sir," the man said softly, "Please go straight ahead into the grand parlor down the hall."

He pointed in the direction and Devon started toward the room following several other mourners. He saw a good friend walking slightly ahead of him. The queen. The "Queen of Crime", as Agatha Christie has been called. He gently tapped her on the shoulder and she turned around. She gave him a great big smile and an equally big hug.

"I figured you'd be here tonight, my boy," she said as she leaned in to kiss him on the cheek. "Sad, sad affair, though, don't you think?"

"I think. On rare occasion," Devon Stone answered with a sly wink. His friend gave him a slight nudge with her shoulder. "Just a quick congratulations are in order, I hear," he whispered as they slowly inched their way toward the parlor. "I just read that you recently won the Grandmaster Award from the Mystery Writers of America. Well, done, m'lady...well done."

She waved him off.

"Just a silly piece of trivia that someone will take note of decades from now," she huffed. "By the way, you must come see my latest play. Well, when it opens, that is," and she chuckled. "*Witness for the Prosecution*. It's going to open sometime in October. They haven't started rehearsals yet but I love the cast they've chosen."

"I shall be there on opening night, my friend," he answered. "It's a solemn promise. Not to make light of *this* somber situation tonight, but I can't help but think about Fleck and *your* last novel, *Destination Unknown*. He's arrived at one."

Agatha Christie shot him a withering look.

"You are a *very* bad boy," she said, swatting him on his shoulder.

They arrived at the grand parlor and it was, indeed, grand. If more than a bit overwhelming. A huge, open room with ornate gilt-framed old paintings on every wall, antique credenzas, cabinets filled with crystal glassware of every type along with dozens of hand-blown glass paperweights, and a handmade Chesterfield sofa covered in rich, red, silk brocade. The hardwood parquet floors were partially covered by beautiful oriental carpets with the predominant colors of scarlet and indigo blue. In the center of the ceiling hung an enormous crystal chandelier with lights that resembled flickering candles. The walls were covered in deep red silk.

"A touch of red might help, don't you think?" Devon whispered into Agatha Christie's ear.

"I think. On rare occasion," she answered back, nudging him gently on the shoulder.

The central part of the room was filled with folding chairs arranged neatly facing a podium. A huge framed photographic portrait of Samuel Fleck rested on an easel next to the podium. Enormous bouquets of white gladioli flanked the portrait, with another similar bouquet on the opposite side of the podium. A cellist sat off to the side playing soft, somber chamber music. Devon Stone and Agatha Christie looked at one another with raised eyebrows.

The first few rows of chairs were filled with mourners, with others scattered about in the other seats.

"As you know, I detest large crowds, so I'm sitting as far back as possible," said Agatha. "I want to make a hasty exit when this show is over."

"I see my publisher up there in the middle," Devon answered. "Excuse me, my friend, but I'll go sit with him. It was grand seeing you again, even considering the circumstances. But then, you seem to relish dealing with death," he said with another sly wink.

"But only on the printed page, young man. Go."

Devon Stone slid into the empty chair next to James Flynn, his London-based publisher and they politely shook hands. A few seconds later Lydia Hyui took a seat next to Devon.

"What a pleasant surprise," he said with a broad smile. "I didn't realize that you might have been invited to this thing as well."

"I wasn't," answered Lydia, nodding toward his publisher. "James contacted me and thought I might like to attend. Fleck's last few books have just been collecting dust on the shelves in my shop, but he had conducted several readings there over the past year or so. Didn't generate many sales, but I liked the poor man. He was sweet. I guess his son didn't know about my shop or me. I wasn't offended, mind you. It really wasn't an oversight."

"Well, I must say that I am delighted to see you again, Lydia," Devon said, again with a mischievous wink. "It's been awhile. We must get together for some…tea, or something soon."

Lydia Hyui rolled her eyes and concealed a chuckle.

As if on cue, the cellist stopped playing.

The conversational buzz in the room suddenly became silent as a man strode into the room and up to the podium. Wearing a stylish bespoke suit of dark gray linen that obviously had its beginning on Savile Row, the tall, extremely handsome man, looking to be in his late thirties, cleared his throat. He adjusted his crisp black and white houndstooth silk necktie and smiled slightly as he looked out over the audience with his intense dark brown eyes.

"Good evening, ladies and gentlemen. I'm sure most of you have absolutely no idea who I might be. I'm Jeremy Fleck. Son of the deceased."

Silence.

He turned slowly for a lingering glance at the portrait by his side. He sighed and cleared his throat once again. Devon Stone couldn't tell if the man was nervous or merely emotional considering the situation.

"I sincerely appreciate your attendance this evening," he continued. "Neither my father nor I believed in much folderol regarding formal funeral rituals and such."

There was an uncomfortable shuffling of people in their chairs.

"We had strange beliefs, I suppose, according to many. *He* certainly did, any way. But I felt that an evening to honor my beloved father was in order. I regret that he and I had not been closer over the past couple of years. But he was a decent and loving father when convenient and I owe him respect in return. I know that he had many devoted readers throughout his impressive career. Unfortunately, their devotion turned away from him following his past few publications." A short pause as he glanced around the audience. "Taking one's own life is both a brave and cowardly way to make an exit."

More uncomfortable rustling and shuffling.

"Where the *hell* is this tribute going?" James Flynn whispered softly into Devon's ear.

"But, sadly…very sadly," Jeremy Fleck continued, "I am here to make a startling confession. To you. To the world. I feel certain, now, that I am the one responsible for my father's suicide."

Dead silence in the room. All eyes on the young man at the podium.

Jeremy Fleck inhaled deeply, held it briefly and then exhaled slowly through his mouth before speaking.

"My father, Samuel Fleck, did *not* write those unsuccessful books the past couple of years. I did."

Gasps from the audience. Devon Stone and James Flynn stared at each other in disbelief.

"Father had reached a point when the ideas stopped coming to him. He tried to write but nothing worked, in his mind. Nothing seemed right."

Devon Stone recognized that feeling.

"Father knew that I had toyed with the idea of writing fiction throughout the years and that I had a couple of manuscripts," Jeremy Fleck continued with his confession. "I showed them to my father and he gave me encouragement and some critiques. But I had an idea. In retrospect it may have been a grievous one. I was an unknown. He was not. Being that he seemed to be suffering from writer's block I suggested, with a few alterations from him, that he publish them as his own. I felt really and truly sorry for the guy."

"Preposterous!" Devon Stone whispered back into James Flynn's ear. "This is news to me. What writer would *ever* do such a thing?"

James Flynn just stared in disbelief at the young man standing at the podium.

Jeremy Fleck, brushing back a lock of his wavy dark brown hair that had fallen across his brow, rambled on for another five minutes with his combination of sorrowful confession and forthright, if somewhat ambiguous praise of his deceased father, but Devon's thoughts vacillated between utter shocked surprise and total disbelief. *What is the point of this confession?* Devon thought. *Why now?*

Whatever Jeremy Fleck was trying to sell to this audience, Devon Stone wasn't buying it. He was not one to make snap judgments about people but he was willing to make an exception with Jeremy Fleck. Something about the man's demeanor almost bordering on haughtiness set Devon on edge.

The bizarre evening continued on for another agonizing thirty minutes, with friends of Samuel Fleck speaking briefly at the podium following Jeremy's invitation to do so. Finally the bereaved son thanked everyone for attending and, with tears streaming down his cheeks, he bid everyone a good night and safe travels. Most of the attendees, still in a state of shock, silently filed out of the room while a few of them went forward to offer condolences to Jeremy Fleck, shaking his hand and patting him on the shoulder. Devon Stone sat back, watched and listened to one pathetic platitude after the other. And rolled his eyes. *I'm so sorry for your loss. He's in God's hands now. A talent gone too soon. If there is anything I can do. You're in our thoughts and prayers.*

"I'm leaving, Stone," said James Flynn as he got up. "I'm speechless."

"So am I, James. Speechless, that is. But I'm not leaving just yet. I want a few words with that young man. Care to join me, Lydia?"

"Yes, as a matter of fact, I would," answered Lydia Hyui, shaking her head.

# 9

Devon waited until the last of the mourners had left the front of the room and then he started walking toward Jeremy Fleck.

The cellist packed up his gear and was leaving the room as another man entered to start taking down the folding chairs.

"What are you thinking of doing...or saying, Devon?" whispered Lydia.

"I'll know when I get there," he whispered his answer.

"Good evening and thank you *so* much for coming, Mr. Stone," said Jeremy Fleck quickly extending his hand.

"You know who I am, then" said a surprised Devon Stone.

Jeremy Fleck laughed.

"Half the world does, don't they?" Fleck responded. "Father spoke highly of you often...whenever I was around, that is. And your photo is on the back of every one of your books, right? I may have been out of the country for many years, but I haven't left the planet."

"I wish that I had been a better friend to your late father, young man," said Devon trying to sound earnest. "I was devastated when I heard about his...death. I understand that you live in the orient somewhere, correct?"

"Yes, I've been living in Hong Kong for several years."

Lydia Hyui's eyes lit up.

"Seriously?" she replied.

"Oh, I'm so sorry," Devon quickly interjected. "Please forgive my rudeness. Jeremy, please meet a very good friend of mine, Lydia Hyui."

Jeremy's reaction to her name was slight.

"It's a pleasure to meet you Miss…Hughes, is it?"

There was a sudden loud noise behind them that made Lydia jump and let out a little yelp. A man was folding up the chairs and leaning them against one of the walls. A couple chairs had slid down and hit the bare hardwood flooring. The embarrassed man apologized and went about his business.

"Yes, well, it sounds like Hughes but it's Hyui and it's spelled H-Y-U-I. It's Chinese. I actually moved here from Hong Kong just a couple years ago," said Lydia Hyui, regaining her composure following the jarring noise behind her. "My kid brother still lives there."

"Oh, really?" was Jeremy Fleck's only answer.

Devon couldn't tell if that reply was one of disinterest or curiosity.

"Yes, his name is Jian Hyui. He performs there in the Cantonese Opera. Perhaps you've heard of him?"

Jeremy Fleck's pause was long enough to puzzle Devon further.

"Can't say that I have," responded Fleck looking back and forth between Lydia and Devon with a polite smile. "It's a very large and hectic city, as you well know. And I don't attend the opera."

"Your father's death upset me greatly, Jeremy," said Devon, again trying to sound earnest and saddened without be overly morose about it. "I'm going to ask what may seem like an insensitive question at this time. But, as a mystery writer, my curiosity has been piqued. There has been very little attention in the media about your father's suicide, which sort of surprised me considering his notoriety. The press didn't mention anything about a suicide note. There usually *is* one. Did Samuel leave one, by any chance?"

Devon was met with a cold, lingering stare. And then a slight nod. And another polite smile.

"Oh. Well. Why, yes, as a matter of fact he *did* leave a note of sorts. It was tucked beneath a photograph of me that he happened to have on his desk in his office."

"And the authorities didn't report that to the press at any time?" asked

Devon. "You know how us Brits just love juicy stuff like that. If the Queen Mother gets soused on gin and Dubonnet or if our beloved Queen herself should swat a fly on her husband's bum us commoners want hear about it, you know?"

Another pause.

"The authorities knew nothing of it. I took it to be more a note of apology and not necessarily a quote-unquote suicide note. I also had the thought that perhaps it was not yet finished. That maybe he still wanted to add to it. It was a very pathetic, and unnerving note and I didn't want father's loyal fans to be upset about it. It was a bit too revealing. You can appreciate that, I'm sure. It was very personal. Yes, I should have paid more attention to his moods, but I visited rarely these days. I also knew he had serious bouts of depression over the years. There was a full moon the night of his suicide. Purely unrelated coincidence perhaps. But I've read studies that severe depression and suicide rates increase around that occurrence every month. Were you aware of that?"

Yes, Devon Stone was aware of that but remained silent, simply nodding his head and cocking his head to one side.

A long, uncomfortable pause. Too long.

"Would you be interested in reading it?" asked Fleck, really hoping that Devon Stone would decline. "The note, I mean."

"Oh my goodness. If you wouldn't mind," answered Devon. "I promise. My lips are sealed. I'll never say a bloody word to the press."

"It's still up in his office. Do you have a moment? I shall get it and be right back."

"That would be awfully decent of you, Jeremy," said Devon, his sarcasm concealed beautifully. "I'd be honored if you would share it."

Jeremy Fleck left the room and Devon heard his footfalls going up the long wooden staircase.

"Just what do you suppose is going on here?" asked a confused-looking Lydia Hyui.

"Unlike Marc Anthony with Caesar," answered Devon, shaking his head slowly, "Fleck was here to neither bury nor praise his father. I sincerely wish that my instincts weren't as acute. From the first moments upon hearing about Samuel's so-called suicide I was skeptical. Perhaps I'll be proven wrong. I *hope* that I'll be proven wrong."

Ten long minutes later, Jeremy Fleck reentered the room and walked slowly toward Devon and Lydia.

"I apologize," he said, "I thought I had placed it in one of my dresser drawers upstairs but I couldn't locate it right away. It took me a moment or two to remember exactly what I had done with it."

He held out the handwritten note to Devon.

"No need to apologize, lad, this is awfully decent of you to share this painful situation with us. Before I even glance at it, is this *really* way too personal? Should I have declined your offer to let me read it?"

Jeremy Fleck smiled halfheartedly, shrugged his shoulders and let out a long sigh.

"No, that's alright, Mr. Stone. He valued your friendship. Yes, it *is* very personal and, I must admit that I sobbed when I read it. And I may sob again once you two leave tonight. I'm sorry, but I really miss my father *so* much right now."

Devon Stone still wasn't buying it.

He smiled back at Jeremy and began reading, with Lydia looking over his shoulder.

*My dear, dear Jeremy. Please forgive me and, above all, please do not despise me for what I've done in the past. I am a failure. I may not have always shown it, but I have loved you with all my heart. I am a failure. I let you down. I let my faithful readers down. I am a failure. I let your sweet mother down when I couldn't save her from the black fog. I am a failure. I betrayed you and betrayed your dear, dear mother time and time again. The pain that I feel in my soul just seems too great to bear at times. I have lied so much throughout my entire life and I've been so ashamed to tell the truth. But I shall tell the truth, as painful as it might be. I promise. But I am still a failure and you know it.*

The note ended abruptly, as if the writer still had more to say. Just as Jeremy Fleck had inferred.

Devon Stone stopped reading, sighed deeply, and handed the note back to Jeremy Fleck. He heard someone walk up behind them and turned to look.

An attractive young woman was standing silently. She looked to be in her late twenties or early thirties, and conservatively dressed all in black as though for a funeral. She nodded and smiled sweetly.

"Oh, my," said Jeremy Fleck, " How nice of you to come, Miss Barnes. I didn't see you in the crowd earlier."

Devon and Lydia smiled at the young woman.

"Devon, Lydia," said Fleck making the introduction. "This young lady is Beth Barnes. She is…or, rather, she *was* my father's part-time housekeeper. She had the misfortune of finding my poor father after he had committed suicide."

Beth Barnes shook hands gently with both Devon and Lydia.

"Nice to meet you both," she said with a slight bow. She smiled and took a step back. "I don't want to interrupt your conversation with Mr. Fleck," she said, almost apologetically. "I just wanted to extend my condolences once again. Mr. Fleck and I haven't really had the opportunity to simply reflect on the tragic event."

"No problem, Miss Barnes," answered Devon. "We were about to leave. Thank you, Jeremy, for sharing this painful note with us. I can understand why you didn't want to share it with the world. It *does* appear a bit too personal. And perhaps painful."

"Thank you, Mr. Stone. And thank both of you for coming this evening. Perhaps we'll meet again sometime."

"Perhaps we will, Jeremy. Perhaps we will," said Devon Stone fixing his stare directly into the young man's eyes.

Jeremy Fleck and Beth Barnes watched as Devon Stone and Lydia Hyui walked out of the room, heard them as the walked down the long hallway and heard the front door close behind them. They turned and smiled at each other. They embraced and held a long, sensual kiss.

"Well, my dear," Jeremy said when their lips parted, "Did you happen to hear any of that conversation? What an unexpected surprise *that* was. Jesus Christ. What were the bloody chances?"

# 10

Devon Stone and Lydia Hyui sat close to each other in the taxicab ride back to his house. Lydia's arms were folded across her chest. She had been looking out the window but she turned abruptly to face him.

"Fleck should have at least served us all wine tonight along with his *pitiful* confession," Lydia said suddenly with a disgusted tone to her voice.

Devon laughed out loud.

"Honestly! And that housekeeper, by the way. Beth whatever her name was. She seems awfully young, doesn't she? And attractive," Lydia continued. "Didn't strike me as the housekeeper type. Do you suppose she and Samuel might have had something going on?"

"Beth Barnes," Devon replied, "and I *seriously* doubt that. Among my many instincts, I can guarantee that wasn't one of them."

"So what are your *other* instincts telling you now, Devon?" she asked.

"Oh, a couple of things, Lydia. A couple of things. I have neither right nor reason to contact the medical examiner at this point. Not even sure if he would be allowed to tell me. But I sense that something is definitely afoot. Maybe I'll be proven wrong in the very near future. I have *no* idea where young Mr. Fleck was going with that full moon bullshit. A lot of mumbo-jumbo, if you ask me. Samuel Fleck was an odd duck, to be sure, and had many issues…but being a werewolf was certainly *not* one of them. A suicidal werewolf, no less."

Lydia Hyui giggled.

"Oh, stop," she said swatting him on the shoulder. "Be serious. Just because he mentioned full moon? Werewolf. Honestly, Devon, sometimes your imagination just needs to be reined in. *Werewolf.* Oh, good grief!"

He chuckled.

"Well of course you know I was being facetious. Besides, Samuel didn't look *anything* like Lon Chaney. However," Devon continued, "*one* thing made my ears prick up."

"And that would have been?"

"You made a brief mention of your brother and Fleck reacted. It was slight, but I caught it. And also you spelled out your last name when you thought he had misinterpreted it. It would be an extremely strange and probably highly unlikely coincidence, I must admit, if he *does* happen to know your brother. Or at least to know about him. But seriously, what would the chances be?"

"He could have been lying, of course, but he said that he *didn't* know about my brother," Lydia replied.

"Actually, he did *not* say that. You asked if, by any chance, he had heard of your brother. His response was 'can't say that I have'. Two different things, wouldn't you agree? And he wouldn't have been lying."

"Hmmm…well, you're right. And, of course, I have to agree with you about the highly unlikely chance that he knows anything about my brother. So you think he *may* have been lying?"

"Oh, I can't go quite that far. Yet," answered Devon. "But I just can't be sure that he was telling the whole truth. A matter of semantics, I suppose."

"Interesting," Lydia said, sitting back. "I'm intrigued. Incidentally, I don't know if it was planned or by sheer accident that all the flowers in those enormous displays were white. White is the color of mourning in my culture, not black. Did you know that?"

"Of course I do, my dear. I'm a writer and I know things."

Lydia Hyui giggled and shook her head.

"I've heard you say that *so* often that it's become a cliché, Devon. Do you have any idea what Jeremy Fleck does? I assume whatever it is it's in Hong Kong."

"I do *not* know and, as Gable once famously said, frankly my dear, I don't give a damn."

They rode along quietly for a few moments, both of them thinking back on tonight's very bizarre event.

"Well, speaking of my brother," Lydia Hyui finally broke the silence, "I'm flying down to Hong Kong at the end of next week. He will be performing in a debut performance of a *spectacular* opera. A thought just struck me. If you've got nothing better to do, would you care to join me?"

"Opera? Good lord! I'm not a big fan of musicals, Lydia…unless, of course, someone is murdered in it."

Lydia couldn't help laughing so hard she nearly choked.

"Devon Stone, you are incorrigible. Honestly, I *do* know that characters will die in this one. Very theatrically, of course. There will be a lot of simulated battle scenes. I know the story well. They've been in rehearsal for several weeks."

"Hummph," muttered Devon, thinking for a moment before he continued. "You know what? I haven't been to Hong Kong since I was a kid. Went there with my late parents. Nothing better to do? Ha! It might be a pleasant diversion, though. But *opera*?"

Lydia laughed once again.

"To be perfectly honest, Devon, Chinese opera *can* be very painful to western ears. Loud, shrill, dissonant music and weird-sounding voices."

Devon thought about her offer for a few moments.

"I repeat. You know what? Perhaps I *do* need a change of scenery for a bit. Maybe get my creative juices flowing again. All right, my dear, I *will* accompany you to Hong Kong. But won't I be an imposition? I assume you'll be staying with your brother there, right?"

"God, no!" Lydia responded loudly. "Jian lives in a horrid little flat in an awful part of town. I'm surprised that he hasn't been mugged or killed around there yet. I worry about him constantly. He's such a sweet, gentle and naïve soul. I will absolutely *not* be staying with him. I've already booked a suite at the Peninsula Hotel."

It was nearing dawn and a solitary figure, wearing a long indigo-blue coat along with a conical straw hat, suddenly stopped walking down a dark alleyway in Kowloon Walled City.

Hesitation.

A sound.

Someone else breathing. Someone a little too close behind. Someone with evil intent.

The intended mugging victim swiveled around quickly, aimed low on the attacker's body, lunged forward, swiftly slicing across the torso hoping to separate the man from his penis.

He nearly succeeded.

Within seconds the malefactor was disemboweled and beheaded.

Although he never thought that a medical term actually existed defining the odd sensation he felt as his adrenaline started pumping and his heart started racing, when Hyui swung his deadly blades at his mugger he was experiencing tachypsychia, a neurological condition that distorts the perception of time. To him, all of his precise, swift actions appeared to be in slow motion. But to his attacker, the lethal actions were over practically before he even realized what was happening.

Jian Hyui, with hands still quivering, casually strolled back to his flat, carefully washed and then coated his two long blades thoroughly with protective mineral oil, undressed and climbed into his rickety bed. He drifted into sleep as tears slowly rolled down his cheeks and the aroma of Tiger Balm filled his nostrils.

And then the dreams began once again.

# 11

Depending upon how one felt about it, landing at the Kai Tak Airport in Hong Kong could be an exciting experience or a terrifying one. Because of its locale, with water on three sides of the runways, 2,000-foot mountains and residential apartment complexes to the northeast of the airport, airplanes had to fly in over Victoria Harbour and make a sharp 47° right-hand turn and then quickly drop for the final approach. A white-knuckle approach for some passengers, a thrill ride for others. Probably there has been more than one nervous passenger over the years that have wondered, while coming in for a landing, if this is perhaps the one flight they should *not* have taken. The airport was, at one time, ranked as the 6th most dangerous airport in the world.

The stewards went up and down the aisle reminding everyone to securely fasten their seatbelts as the four-engine BOAC Argonaut Speedbird aircraft was about to land. It had been a long flight; the passengers were tired and eager to deplane.

After going through customs and baggage claim, Lydia Hyui and Devon Stone stepped through the arrival door into the terminal. An older, white-haired man dressed impeccably in a chauffer's uniform, held up his hand and gave a gentle nod and a wave. Lydia smiled at him and waved back.

"Now, Mr. Stone," she said with a smile, "you are in for a treat. Hello, Jason," she said as they approached the gentleman.

"Good afternoon, Miss Hyui," said Jason Chang. "Welcome back to Hong Kong. It's always a pleasure to see you."

The chauffer offered to take their pieces of luggage and then turned to walk away. Lydia and Devon followed.

Devon Stone didn't know what to say, but that would change within minutes.

"I know you like motor vehicles, don't you?" asked Lydia. "You seem to be very proud of *yours* and always keep it spotless. Just wait," and she smiled broadly.

They walked through a part of the airport that appeared to be more secluded than the rest, with hardly any passengers. Devon wasn't sure what to expect. They finally stepped through doors leading to what appeared to be a very private parking area.

Devon stopped in his tracks, his mouth agape, as Jason Chang opened the doors of their vehicle.

"That?" Devon gasped. "We're going in *that*?"

He recognized it immediately.

*That* was an immaculately restored, glistening, black 1934 Rolls-Royce Phantom II.

"Close your mouth, Devon," chuckled Lydia, "I think you're drooling."

Jason Chang ushered them into the gorgeous vehicle, put their small pieces of luggage into the boot, and then climbed into the driver's seat. Off they went...in grand style.

Twenty minutes later the car turned into the entryway of the prestigious Peninsula Hotel, in the district of Tsim Sha Tsui. It drove around the rectangular fountain in the center of the forecourt and halted at the front doors. If they had looked in the right direction as they pulled in, they would have seen the harbor terminal for the Star Ferry practically across the street.

Ten minutes later they were ushered into the suite that Lydia Hyui had reserved on the top floor of the six-floor hotel.

Devon Stone walked over to the floor-to-ceiling windows and gazed out across the beautiful Victoria Harbour and over to Hong Kong Island on the other side. He glanced further up, recognizing Victoria Peak, the highest hill on Hong Kong Island.

"This is far more than I had expected, my dear," he said as Lydia came up beside him.

They leaned into each other, melting into a warm embrace.

The dress rehearsal just finished and Lau stood in the wings watching as the singers headed to their dressing rooms. She smiled as Jian Hyui approached, and applauded him, adding a slight bow.

"Very well done, young man," she said. "I am *extremely* impressed. Your performance will be far more than I had expected. You have obviously been practicing. Your movements and grace are perfection. Quick as a cat out of a sack."

Obviously Lau enjoyed using that expression.

Jian Hyui chuckled silently to himself, smiled and gave his instructor a very deep bow from his waist.

"I am honored to have been your student, Sifu Lau," he responded.

The telephone in the suite rang, breaking the mood. Leaving Devon naked and aroused in the bed, Lydia got up and answered the phone in Mandarin.

*Timing is everything,* he thought to himself shaking his head.

He listened as she was obviously enjoying the conversation, having switched, now, to speaking in English. She laughed and said her goodbye as she hung up.

She returned to the side of the bed but made no move to get in there with an anxiously awaiting Devon.

"That was my brother, Jian, just now. He made the astute assumption that my flight was on schedule and that I was here. His rehearsal finished an hour ago and he is ravenous. I offered to treat him to dinner, as I always do when I arrive, which I knew he would readily accept. You, Devon, will be a surprise to him. I hadn't told him I'd be bringing you to Hong Kong."

"Will he be upset or anything?" asked Devon, a bit concerned. "Does he know that we have a...well...a bit of a close friendship going on?"

"Oh, don't be silly. Of course he won't be upset. This is 1955, not the Dark Ages, you know. We're all adults, now, aren't we? Yes, he *does* know that I have been seeing a gentleman. I've told him your name, that's all. He's very progressive in his own simple way. Shy as a blushing virgin schoolgirl, to be sure, but very open-minded."

"I find that very difficult to believe. I don't think that I've ever met a performer of any kind who is shy, Lydia. They are usually such extroverts that it's painful at times," and he chuckled.

"Aside from when he is onstage performing, I honestly believe that he suffers from what you might call severe social anxiety. Don't be surprised if he remains very silent during dinner. He's certainly *not* the most loquacious person in the world."

She thought for a moment before continuing.

"And...well...Jian is...hmmm...how can I put this delicately? Jian is more comfortable performing as a female character on stage than actually being himself as a man offstage. I honestly don't believe that he's queer, as they say, but his masculine side has always been somewhat eclipsed."

"Well," smiled Devon Stone, " *that's* putting it delicately?"

"And," laughed Lydia, "if you were expecting a grand, sumptuous Chinese meal for our first night here in Hong Kong, forget about it. Jian requested a grand, sumptuous *western* meal tonight. Actually, it's one of *my* favorite places here, as well. We'll have to take a ferry to get to the other side of the harbor. You'll *love* this place, I'm sure. Jimmy's Kitchen. Very British, surprisingly. And just about the best steak house in the city. If you happen to be in the mood for prime rib, which I know you like, be prepared."

"I assume, then," Devon said with a sigh as he rolled over and stood up from the bed, "that now we should get dressed for dinner."

Lydia Hyui smiled and winked, as she looked him up and down.

"We'll resume what we just started when we get back later tonight, dear boy. We shall be each other's dessert."

Devon Stone snickered.

"Along with a fortune cookie?"

# 12

After arriving on Hong Kong Island by the Star ferry, Devon Stone and Lydia Hyui strolled along, arm in arm, down Wyndham Street as rickshaws, busses and taxicabs whizzed by. Devon looked especially handsome in navy blazer, gray gabardine slacks, and an open-collared pale blue linen shirt with a burgundy and navy ascot tucked in at the neck. His French cuff sleeves extended perfectly from his jacket and were adorned by small square gold cufflinks engraved with the initials DS. DS for Daniel Stein, Devon's late, beloved father whose cuff links these once had been. They were Devon's favorite cuff links although he had at least a dozen pairs. Lydia looked gorgeous in a fashionable, intricately tailored, form-fitting cheongsam with purple and emerald floral accents and with a long slit on the right side, revealing a very shapely leg. Her long, shiny black hair was swept up into a twist held together by a centuries-old jade comb. They had complimented each other's attire before leaving their hotel room and they each agreed that they made a very striking couple.

They turned down a short pedestrian passageway between two buildings and then walked down the steps that led into the restaurant. The popular dining facility was actually located in the lower level of the South China Building. He reacted with a huge smile because he could already smell the sizzling steaks.

Lydia stopped just before they reached the door. She put her hand on Devon's arm.

"Oh, as I mentioned when we were talking earlier about my brother. Remember that I didn't tell him you were here with me in Hong Kong."

"Remember? My dear, I can never forget...if *you* will remember," said Devon with a shrug.

"But I honestly don't know if he actually knows *who* you are. By that I mean, that you're an author of murder mysteries. I told you that he is a very sweet, gentle, and sensitive soul. Aside from this role that he's undertaking in *Hua Mulan*, I doubt that violence of any kind has ever entered his mind. I'm sure that he doesn't even kill spiders."

"Oh, great," Devon responded. "Should I perhaps let on that I write mawkish poetry...or sentimental romance novels?"

Lydia giggled.

"We'll just play it by ear, but I wanted to give you a bit of a heads-up."

"Well, then," said Devon. "Let's head *in*."

The evening would *not* go as Lydia Hyui had anticipated. Not at all.

They were greeted by the smiling maître d as they stepped into the elegant, popular restaurant. It was dimly lit, wood-paneled, with plush, deep red upholstered chairs and matching red carpeting.

"Good evening, Miss Hyui," said the tuxedoed gentleman, with a slight bow. "It is always a distinct pleasure to have you dining with us. Your brother has already arrived and is at the table awaiting you. Please follow me."

And they followed.

The restaurant was crowded and abuzz with conversations in various languages and dialects.

As they approached the table, Jian Hyui stood up with a warm smile and reached out to embrace his sister.

"Nǐ hǎo, jiějiě," he said, "Wǒ xiǎngniàn nǐ, *hello, sister, I've missed you.*"

"And I've missed you as well, Jian. So glad that your opera gave me a good reason to come for this visit. I have a surprise for you, and this..."

"And is this the world-famous Devon Stone?" Jian Hyui interrupted, extending his hand to Devon.

Lydia Hyui was aghast.

"I was hoping you would be bringing him," he continued, bowing slightly from the waist to Devon and shaking his hand. It was a very firm handshake, at that. So firm that Devon was momentarily taken aback. He had been expecting perhaps a limp, almost effeminate handshake. "I am so pleased that you have come too and I have several questions. But sit down, please," he laughed, motioning to their seats. "We simply cannot enjoy our meals standing up all evening, can we? People will stare."

Lydia, with raised eyebrows, looked at Devon and he simply shrugged his shoulders as he held out the chair for her to sit. When seated, she leaned back into her comfortable chair.

"So, then, you *do* know who Devon Stone is?" She was still a bit befuddled.

"I do, dear sister, I do. And, Mr. Stone, I have so enjoyed reading many of the thrilling novels that you wrote. I am deeply honored that now I actually get to meet you."

Lydia Hyui was so taken aback by her brother's behavior that she was momentarily speechless.

"I certainly appreciate that, Jian," Devon answered, still a bit confused about what Lydia had told him earlier.

Without the slightest hesitation, Jian Hyui launched right into a conversation, one that Devon Stone would never have anticipated.

"I *never* anticipated getting the opportunity to discuss your writings in person. Forgive me if I gush too much or am too blunt. We can hold off and discuss this further during our dinner if you care to, but I must say, Mr. Stone, I was intrigued the most by one of your writings a couple books ago. The one about the revenge killings."

"Ah, you must be referring to *The Fallen*, right?" responded Devon.

"Yes, that is the one. Yes. *The Fallen*."

Devon Stone chuckled.

"I'm sure you might not be aware of it, Jian, but that one generated the most controversy regarding my loyal readers. I got more blowback from that one than any of my other books. Many were shocked by the reasons for the killings and by the violence. I received countless pieces of hate mail as a result."

*The Fallen*, to which they were referring, was a Devon Stone thriller about the gang rape and subsequent murder of a young college coed by several of her drunken classmates, none of whom had ever been implicated or charged for the crime by the authorities. Although they had each been questioned about the heinous tragedy, they had each pledged a code of secrecy to baffle the investigation, rehearsed their respective false stories beforehand with each other and had, supposedly, rock solid alibis. Based on certain clues she secretly and steadfastly unearths, the older sister of the victim quietly tracks down the perpetrators and, one by one, and in very graphic ways, tortures and murders them. The book, however, did not end well for the sister.

"What shocked *me* the most…and saddened me," said Jian, "was the fact that you had the heroine die at the end. The murders she committed, although for revenge, were justified in my opinion. Yes, illegal, needless to say, but those young men were reprehensible, having no scruples whatsoever. Was it moral ambiguity on your part as the author? Are you, too, opposed to revenge killings?"

Lydia Hyui stared at her brother in disbelief.

"Who *are* you?" she asked, "and what have you done with my brother?"

They all laughed.

"Let's just say that sometimes the ends don't always justify the means," Devon Stone said. Devon Stone had just lied.

For reasons he would not…nor *could* not ever divulge, Devon did not *really* answer Jian Hyui's last question. He was taken aback by the odd coincidence. It was this very book, *The Fallen*, which had inspired the younger sister of a murdered Soviet Night Witch to reach out to him for his advice and then to seek his assistance in gaining revenge.

The irony here being that neither man knew they were sitting across the table from each other as murderers.

Devon Stone sat back in his chair, a look of confusion on his face as he turned to look at Lydia Hyui.

*So much for the social amenities*, he thought, *like, how are you, nice to meet you, how was your flight, and isn't the weather wonderful?*

"This is certainly *not* the conversation I was expecting this evening," he said.

And they hadn't even glanced at their menus yet. The evening was still young, with more surprises to come.

A waiter approached the table with a tray of drinks, but no one had ordered anything yet. He carefully set a glass of red wine on the table in front of Lydia; a Brandy Alexander in front of Jian; and a gin and tonic in front of Devon.

Lydia and Devon turned to look at Jian.

"I took the liberty of telling the waiter ahead of time to bring these drinks after you had arrived and we were seated" he said. "I know that Cabernet Sauvignon is my sister's favorite wine and, Mr. Stone, being that you always seem to have your hero in all your books drink gin and tonics, I assumed that that must be *your* drink of choice. Was I correct?"

*This man is just full of surprises,* Devon Stone thought to himself.

Oh, but there's more.

An hour and a half later, after a few rounds of drinks and roasted prime rib of beef all around the table, the satiated trio was ready for coffee.

The dinnertime conversation topics had bounced around from the upcoming opera, to several of Devon Stone's past books, and how Lydia Hyui spends her time while away from her bookshop. She and Devon exchanged subtle, sly winks regarding *that* topic.

"Devon, we have discussed this evening," said Jian Hyui, "many of *your* books. I'm sure you might be acquainted with *other* authors in and around the London area, right? I guess, actually, both of you must."

"We both know a few," answered Lydia. "Obviously they may have had book signings from time to time in my shop."

"There isn't actually a Murder Writers Club with secret handshakes and pass codes, or anything like that, Jian," Devon snickered. "But a couple of us *do* keep in touch. I'll call Agatha Christie on her birthday, for example. Not often, but I might run into another author friend sometimes at a pub. Us writers are known to drink. On rare occasion, mind you."

Laughter all around the table.

"Well then, would you happen to know another London-based writer by the name of Samuel Fleck?" asked Jian Hyui.

Both Devon and Lydia stared at each other with this question.

"How odd that you should ask that, Jian," answered Devon. "Do you know his work?"

"Well… yes, I know his work and I know *him*."

"What do you mean by that?" asked Lydia.

"I came across his works only about a couple years ago. You may have mentioned his name on one of your trips here to see me, sister. Something about a book signing at your shop, I think it was. And that he was a very interesting person. I very much enjoyed his first book, *Open Verdict*, and I wrote to him. A simple, gushing fan letter, I guess you might call it. And I was quite surprised and shocked, frankly, that he wrote back. Totally unexpected, mind you. I didn't even know if my little letter of praise would reach him or not. I sent it care of his publishing house and I assume they must have forwarded it on to him. But he must get *hundreds* of such letters. Then I thought that maybe he's the kind of author who responds to *all* of his fan mail."

Devon Stone looked askance.

"And?"

"Well, then, we quickly struck up a long distance friendship. Corresponding by post often. He had sent his postal address to me. As you probably know by now, Lydia, I don't make friends very easily. Hardly at all, for that matter. It was so much easier talking to him in writing, than talking to someone in person. We both became very frank with each other. And one day he surprised me by telling me he was coming to Hong Kong and could we meet."

Devon was flabbergasted.

"Go on," Lydia encouraged.

"We met. We dined. He went to the opera…I was performing. He is a very handsome and charming man, isn't he? We became very…close. He has been back on several trips, and lavishes me with expensive gifts. I'm a very modest and conservative person by nature. Frankly, it embarrasses me. To say that I'm flattered is an understatement. He took me to a fine tailor here in town and had a striking cashmere suit made for me…this very suit I am wearing now, for that matter. He picked out several beautiful silk neckties to accompany it. But for some reason his correspondence has ceased. He hasn't answered my last few letters."

"Oh, no, my poor brother. You have *no* idea, do you?"

Jian Hyui looked at his sister confused.

Devon stepped in. He didn't hesitate.

"Samuel Fleck committed suicide a month or so ago."

Jian Hyui gasped; putting his hands to his mouth as tears quickly came to his eyes.

"Your sister and I, Jian, attended a memorial service for him just last week. It was a strange one; I'll give you that. It was conducted, so to speak, by his son."

"Wait," said Jian Hyui wiping away a few tears. "I don't understand. A son? Samuel had a son? He never told me that!"

Lydia Hyui and Devon Stone again stared at each other.

*What the fuck is going on here?* Devon thought to himself.

# 13

"When you said, Jian," asked Lydia, "that you and Samuel were 'close', exactly *how* close? If you don't think that's too impertinent of a question."

Jian Hyui, still with tears in his eyes, blushed as a slight smile crossed his face.

"I know what you are inferring, sister. I can also guess what you might have been thinking about me for all these years. To answer your question first…our friendship was strictly platonic. Samuel wanted it to be otherwise. That's why I was shocked to discover he had a son. Regarding my *own* feelings? Ah, well…that's another matter. I actually haven't figured myself out quite yet."

Devon Stone, clearly embarrassed by the direction of this conversation, pushed his chair back from the table.

"This is getting a bit *too* personal for me at the moment, Lydia and Jian. I shall seek out the gentlemen's room while you two sort out this topic."

"That's fine, Devon," said Jian, "unless you *really* need to use the facilities, I'm comfortable with the way our conversation is going. Maybe fodder for a book or two of yours in the future. Who knows, right?"

"No, I really *do* need the facilities," said Devon as he stood.

Lydia waited until Devon had departed. She watched as he walked away, then turned and smiled at Jian. She reached over and placed a gentle hand on his forearm.

"I'm sorry, my dear brother, I don't need to pry into your private life. That was shameful on my part. I am neither judging nor criticizing you in any way. You must know that."

"No, no. Please don't worry about it, sweet Lydia. I may not have been able to conceal it as well as I hoped, but I have had stirrings for both genders. I've acted upon none of them. Emotions are confusing things, aren't they?"

Jian Hyui had no intention of telling his sister that a mysterious man on the Star Ferry had murdered someone who had tormented him and lusted after him for a long time. Nor would he ever tell her about his activities long after dark within Kowloon Walled City. *What kind of person have I become?* Jian thought. *A psychopath? A sociopath? Serial killer!* He had committed a heinous crime. Several of them. He kept waiting for the damning sense of guilt to creep into his tormented soul. But neither guilt nor remorse ever came. Yet.

"Moving aside from that sad, tragic situation regarding my dear friend Samuel, sister, the training for this particular opera has changed me in surprising ways. I once was a timid little mouse of a man. You may not believe it, but now I feel as though I can slay dragons."

They sat in silent thought now as they awaited Devon's return to the table.

Lydia Hyui was confused. Although it had been quite a while since her last visit to Hong Kong, and the two of them had communicated often on the telephone, why had her brother not mentioned his friendship with Samuel Fleck until tonight? And his normally shy, unassuming demeanor was now apparently nonexistent. Where had it gone? And why? And what took its place?

Twenty minutes later, the trio casually strolled side-by-side back toward the Star Ferry pier. The light from a full moon flickered and danced across the waters of Victoria Harbour as they approached.

Lydia Hyui's mind was swirling with conflicted thoughts about her brother's uncharacteristic behavior earlier this evening and Samuel Fleck.

Devon Stone's mind was racing with conflicted thoughts about his departed friend, Samuel Fleck, and Jian Hyui.

Jian Hyui, also, was thinking about Samuel Fleck…and dragons.

Three hours later, somewhere within the labyrinthine alleyways of Kowloon Walled City Jian Hyui, mimicking the gait of an old woman, walked hunched over slightly. Two men, fellow gang members in one of the Triad groups, stood next to each other back in the shadows. Waiting. It would soon be getting light, although sunlight rarely found its way amongst these closely built pathways. They spotted their potential prey for a swift robbery walking up ahead; they turned to each other and snickered.

"Lǎo tàitài," one of the men said. *Old lady.* Yúchǔn de rén, *stupid person.*

And they both snickered again, stepping out from the shadows and moved swiftly toward their target. The alleyway was so dark that their intended victim now appeared in silhouette, with just the faintest hint of neon light out in front of the figure.

That slowly moving figure, Jian Hyui, suddenly stopped. He was alert. He could sense their presence and picked up the awful, foul smell of one of their breaths. He was ready. His two long knives were well concealed in his loose garments. The two men were right behind him as he swiveled around with so much speed that the men gasped. One of Hyui's long knives sliced right through the left arm of one of the attackers, swiftly severing it from his body. Hyui's second blade sliced straight across the man's face almost at the same time, cracking open the skull and spewing blood, teeth and bone fragments. The man dropped to the ground in a frightening, grotesque heap.

The second man reacted as Jian had expected: with shock and alarm. He turned to run but, consistent with the principle that action beats reaction, Hyui grabbed him around the neck from behind, hooked his arm under the man's chin and effectively cut off the man's windpipe with his left forearm, squeezing tightly. This was a blood choke. He had read about such a maneuver in one of Devon Stone's books. A blood choke cuts off the circulation through the carotid arteries, which supply the appropriate amount of blood to the brain. With his right hand he thrust his long knife into the man's ribs as he squeezed the man's neck even tighter. Within seconds the man collapsed, Hyui not knowing whether it was from asphyxiation or that he had bled out. He let the man fall to the dirty pavement. For good measure he sliced across the man's neck with his blade and then he casually strolled away.

At this point he thought that he *should* surely be exhausted from the long day of rehearsal, dinner with his sister and Devon Stone earlier, and the attack just now. But no, he was energized. Exhilarated, even.

Hours later, by 10 A.M., with the sun brightly shining, a freshly bathed and dressed Jian Hyui walked toward the Star Ferry humming quietly and preparing himself mentally for the long, final dress rehearsal for the opera.

Meanwhile, it was still late evening of the day before on the island of Manhattan.

Veronica Barron and Billy Bennett were enjoying a late dinner at Sardi's. They were among the very few stragglers still remaining as it was approaching closing time. Waiters were hustling around, cleaning tables and chatting amongst themselves. A very tired looking Vincent Sardi, Jr. ambled over to their table for a chat.

"Vince, you look beat," said a concerned Veronica. "What's up?"

"Just a long day, my dear," he answered. "Been here all day and I should have gone home hours ago. Just one of those days, you know? So sorry, though, to hear about your show closing last month."

"Oh, well," Veronica sighed, waving her hand. "It was a fairly decent run. We played four hundred and seventy-nine performances. Unfortunately not in the same league as *South Pacific,* which finally closed last year. But we didn't win any Tonys. And audiences sort of judge that way. They want to see prizewinners. That super-talented little redheaded chickadee who beat me out for that part in *Can-Can* a couple years ago finally got *her* name above the title *of her* new show and it was a damn good one, at that!"

"What ever Lola wants, Lola gets," snickered Vince as he did a wiggly little dance.

They all laughed.

"Yeah," answered Veronica, "and little Lola wanted a Tony. And she won one. I didn't. She deserved it though, I have to admit. She was stunning. But we'll be taking *our* show to London in a couple months for a limited run on the West End. *Nick and Nora* still has a little life left in it for a while anyway. We'll see how the London audiences react."

"When will you two ever have a chance for a honeymoon?" asked Vince.

"Ha!" responded Billy loudly. "Maybe, just *maybe*, when Mrs. Bennett *finally* finishes her run in this show in London we can do what other newlyweds do, although it's almost two years after the fact now."

He turned and pretended to give Veronica an angry scowl, arching an eyebrow.

She stuck out her tongue at him and they all laughed.

Billy Bennett, handsome pilot, World War Two veteran, and Purple Heart recipient, had proposed to Veronica Barron, beautiful singer and actress at this very table at Sardi's a little less than two years ago. They had come here that night to celebrate after hearing that a new Broadway musical, based upon *The Thin Man*, had been written especially for her. They were also celebrating the fact that they had each, along with a couple other friends, escaped danger from a few murderous miscreants. A justice of the peace in New Haven, Connecticut had married Billy and Veronica while the show was there for its out-of-town tryouts. Between rehearsals and then the show actually opening on Broadway, there had been no time for the loving couple to enjoy a relaxing honeymoon.

"And, speaking of London," Veronica said to Billy, "Devon Stone must be traveling somewhere. I've been trying to call him for several days and he never answers the phone. I wanted to let him know that I'll be back in London for a short time."

"Seriously?" laughed Billy Bennett. "He probably heard about your show coming over there and he went into safe hiding. Every time *you're* around he practically gets murdered."

Again, she stuck out her tongue at him.

In an uncharacteristic move, The South China Morning Post, Hong Kong's newspaper of record, had started reporting about the extremely violent and unusually grotesque murders taking place in notoriously crime-ridden Kowloon Walled City. Lau, Hyui's instructor and master in Ving Tsun, took note of these articles with curiosity. And concern. The killings were indiscriminate, meaning that members from various gangs had fallen victim to violent deaths. She knew that turf wars among the Triad syndicates were common and that meat cleavers were often the weapons of choice. Severed limbs were used as a warning. Murders, however, among the gangs were *not* as common. *But.* And there *was* a big "but" with these cases she thought. Something is not quite right. She was afraid to imagine what that *but* was. *But* her suspicions were growing by the hour.

# 14

The final dress rehearsal had gone exceedingly well. Everyone was elated, especially Lau. Aside from the sheer beauty of the pageantry, the martial arts aspect of the performance would be thrilling. Lau still had some reservations about the change she had witnessed in Jian Hyui, however. At least for now she would simply chalk it up to his growing, albeit late-arriving, maturity.

But Lau *was* certain that Hyui's performance would be breathtaking.

"Breathtaking, isn't it?" said Lydia Hyui as she and Devon Stone stood atop Victoria Peak and surveyed the vast vistas all around.

At 1,811 feet tall, this was the highest point on Hong Kong Island and offered 360° views of the city as well as the surrounding islands. The Peak is considered one of the most expensive residential areas in Hong Kong.

The couple had taken the Peak Tram funicular to reach the summit and they decided to play tourist today, with Lydia as the guide.

"This used to be my playground," said Lydia as she swept her arm around the area. "My late parents owned a house over there," she said pointing back to the residential area of the hill, "on Barker Road. *Very* expensive. Jian and I had a great time growing up there. That's why I'm so confused by his desire to live in…well, what I would call squalor. That awful apartment just seems so out of character from what we were used to as children."

"Was he as shy *then* as you claimed he is now?" asked Devon.

"To a degree," answered Lydia, "but he started his training for the opera when he was around ten, I think. He was always the happiest doing that. He really never had any boyhood friends that I can recall. Never interested in sports of any kind."

"I certainly wouldn't have thought him shy at dinner last night," chuckled Devon. "I thought some of his questions were rather bold, didn't you?"

"I'll be frank, I was really taken aback by the change in him since I last visited. It's like he was a completely different person. A refreshing maturity, I suppose, but a bit disconcerting at the same time. And that whole thing with Samuel Fleck has me perplexed also, to say the least. What were the chances? He seemed genuinely distraught by Fleck's suicide."

"And on *that* note, I'm still not convinced that it *was* suicide, but I guess there really isn't anything I can do about it," answered Devon. "Something about his son, Jeremy, just doesn't sit right with me. Being that Samuel was making trips here to Hong Kong, I guess we can assume that he may have been visiting with his son as well as meeting with Jian. We'll just have to stand back and see what the investigations turn up… if anything."

"Honestly, Devon, I think you just need to put that subject to sleep. No pun intended. Unless something else turns up, we just need to accept the fact that Samuel did, indeed, commit suicide. Regarding his trips to Hong Kong, I thought that Jeremy and Samuel were estranged."

Devon Stone merely shrugged his shoulders.

"Come on, Devon. Let's climb up a bit more to the Lions View Point Pavilion. It's where all the old folks come to sit and enjoy the view."

"Hey, are you calling me 'old folks'?"

Lydia giggled.

"Well, you *did* have a birthday not too long ago and you're definitely creeping up on that half-century mark."

Devon smirked.

70

"Hmm…my birthday. Ah, yes, I remember that day fondly. Will we get to celebrate again when we get back to the hotel?"

Lydia giggled again.

"If you're a good boy and promise not to get too tired out before we head to the theatre tonight."

Devon Stone arched his left eyebrow and gave Lydia Hyui a very devilish grin and a lascivious wink.

"I never got my fortune cookie last night," he laughed.

They glanced up into the sky and watched as several large birds swooped and glided on the air currents over the harbor down below.

"Black kites," said Lydia as she pointed up at them. "They're beautiful, aren't they? I've watched dozens of them, at times. This peak is their favorite roosting area."

"I know," Devon said. "I'm a…

"Oh, please don't say it again, Devon," Lydia chuckled.

They walked further up on the peak and looked out over the South China Sea and at several of the surrounding islands. Shielding her eyes from the bright sun, Lydia pointed to one of the larger ones.

"Over there is Pok Liu Chau," she said wistfully. "Also known as Lamma Island. Our parents took us there often when we were growing up. Wonderful seafood restaurants, beautiful beaches and nice hiking trails. Fond memories. Seems so long ago. Too long ago. Life seemed so much simpler back then."

Maybe it was because she was still perplexed by the difference she saw in Jian but, at the moment, Lydia was feeling oddly nostalgic.

"Come on," Devon said, noticing the emotional change in his companion. "Let's head back."

As much as he wanted to, Jian Hyui knew that he couldn't stalk any more dragons in Kowloon Walled City before the big event just a few short hours away. He needed to conserve his strength and especially his voice.

Before he applied his makeup, he stood in front of the mirror in his dressing room and warmed up his voice. It was a fifteen-minute ritual for him, covering the full range of breathing, voicing, resonance, and articulation exercises. He took the two long-bladed knives and practiced with them as well, making a swooshing sound as he swept them around and over his body, lunging forward with each slash.

Backstage was getting crowded with the other performers. The sounds of their vocal exercises resonated throughout the hallways.

It was nearing time.

Jian Hyui sat down at his makeup table and applied his makeup, transforming himself into the maiden Hua Mulan. He stared into the mirror as he finished.

"I'm beautiful," he whispered to himself. "I'm really beautiful."

# 15

The house lights slowly dimmed and the conversational buzz throughout the theater followed suit. Seated in the front row of the mezzanine and glancing around, Devon noted that both he and Lydia were probably the youngest ones in the audience. The opera began with such a sudden startlingly loud crashing of cymbals and a strong beating of drums that it caused many in the audience to react with a slight jolt. When the singing began soon after, Devon Stone was grateful that he knew the performance would last no more than ninety minutes. Although he avoided them, he knew that some Italian operas, and especially German ones, could go on seemingly interminably for several hours.

Ten minutes into the show he thought he might prefer the sounds of pigs being slaughtered, the voices were so jarring.

Twenty minutes into the show he was hoping that a sudden earthquake would empty the theater. He glanced at his TAG Heuer watch and tried willing it to go faster.

He became more fascinated, however, by the elaborate staging and special effects. The stage could revolve 360° and the action began to look very cinematic at times. He was greatly impressed by Jian Hyui, as the female character Hua Mulan, and totally forgot that he was watching a male perform that role. When the Wu Sheng characters (the military roles) appeared he leaned forward, more intent. At this point Hua Mulan had begun impersonating a man and her (his) costumes changed to far more masculine and militaristic, with seemingly heavy armor and helmets. The battle scenes required a high level of martial arts skills involving vigorous exertions of powerful waist and leg movements. The acrobatics were both bazigong (with weapons) and tanzigong (without weapons). There seemed to be more yelling than singing during these scenes. The pulsating lighting effects turned the stage and the performers completely red, simulating violent bloody battles.

The climatic battle scene involved the character of Hua Mulan defeating a horrendously frightening enemy army general, bringing a long war to an end. The mask that the general wore was akin to an ugly, grimacing monster of some sort. Hua Mulan, that is Jian Hyui, took two long-bladed knives, one in each hand, and in slow pantomime motion, launched into a long strenuous battle with the other actor. His/her motions suddenly became more animated and swift. Quick as a cat out of a sack. The sharp clanging sounds of the blades striking each other were frightening. The audience, practically as a whole, gasped loudly as Hua Mulan forcefully, but bloodlessly, vanquished her hideous opponent. Watching from the wings, Lau also gasped loudly as she heard the blades of the long knives clash together just before the ultimate dramatic death of the villain.

Thunderous applause followed the performance and, although standing ovations were a rarity for the opera in Hong Kong, a few patrons bolted straight up out of their seats and held their applauding hands high for the curtain call.

Lydia Hyui turned to Devon.

"Well?" she asked.

"Well," he responded. "I'm impressed by your brother's forceful performance. My ears, however, might take a week to recover from those voices."

Lydia laughed, shaking her head.

"I warned you," she said. "And *I'm* impressed that you managed to sit through the entire show without bolting for the nearest exit!"

The singers all reacted with happy, wide smiles as they bowed for their curtain call. Jian Hyui stood in the center of the line of his fellow performers and bowed in unison graciously. He knew where his sister and Devon were seated and he scoured the first balcony when the house lights came up. His smile widened when he saw them and raised one of the long blades he was still holding toward them as a salute.

His smile dropped immediately thereafter. His gaze had settled on the audience directly in front of him.

He couldn't be sure, but he was almost positive that the Caucasian man sitting in the front row smiling up at him was the same man he had seen on the Star Ferry. The man with the gun.

He held the man's stare.

The man continued to smile at him as he raised his two fingers, tapping them against the side of his forehead and gave Jian Hyui a small salute.

It *is* him!

*Another killer,* thought Jian Hyui as he stared right back at the man, *just like me.*

# PART TWO

---

# OPEN VERDICT

*"If you want to keep a secret, you must hide it from yourself."*
George Orwell

# 16

Jian Hyui lay in his bed, tossing and turning for an hour. And then another hour. He was tormented while awake, and even more so when he dreamed. His dreams haunted him nightly.

*One year earlier...*

A ravishingly beautiful young lady, known to Jian Hyui only as Meili, lived with her aging parents in the apartment directly across the hall from his. They had met one day as they both climbed the rickety stairway to their respective apartments at the same time. They struck up a short conversation. That was highly unusual for Jian, because of his introversion away from the theater. Several other such chance meetings and short conversations followed. He found them enjoyable. He had become smitten by her looks and sweet personality. He was still shy. She was not. She was flirtatious. He was still reserved.

Her father owned one of the many food stalls within the dangerous and foreboding Kowloon Walled City. It was a popular and successful one, serving the best fish balls around. Unbeknownst to many diners in the finest restaurants in Hong Kong, their well-loved dumplings and fish balls often came from such stalls in this crime-laden area.

Meili and Jian sometimes would sit chatting and laughing for hours on the top step of the staircase outside their apartments. Jian, too shy to invite Meili into his flat, Meili not wanting to anger her parents by inviting Jian into hers. He was twenty-five; she was nineteen.

Very late one evening loud shouting and sounds of wailing awakened Jian. He leaped from his bed and cautiously opened the door to his flat. The sounds were coming from across the hall, in the characteristically extremely quiet apartment where Meili resided. Suddenly there was a scream. It was Meili, he knew it.

He banged on the door. No answer, just more loudly shouting voices.

He pounded more strongly on the door, making it rattle and shake on its hinges.

The shouting stopped. Sudden silence.

The door flew open and an old, disheveled man stared out at Jian Hyui. Meili's father, no doubt.

"Zǒu kāi!" he shouted. *Go away!* And the door slammed shut.

He backed slowly across the hallway, entered his flat and started to close his door. Meili rushed in, thrusting open the partially closed door almost throwing Jian Hyui off balance and he nearly fell. Meili slammed the door behind her. He stared at her in disbelief.

Her beautiful face appeared puffy and swollen. Her lips were bloodied. Her blouse was in tatters and her trousers were ripped at the knees.

"Did...did your father do that to you?" Jian asked in horror.

Meili paced around the small entryway, obviously anguished and confused.

"No...no, of course not," she answered through her sobs, trying to catch her breath. She quickly sat down on a small hassock just inside the living room, then just as quickly she stood up again and continued pacing.

"Mǔqīn, *father*, has admonished me from ever going into Kowloon Walled City. Too dangerous for a young girl like me, he said. I never did go. Until tonight. I don't know why, Jian, I just wanted to stroll around to see the shops. To see what it was all about. I didn't know how dark and scary a place it was. I thought he was exaggerating just to scare me from entering. He works in that horrible place, but he must feel safe."

She buried her face in her hands and sobbed openly.

"He warned me of the Triads. How they hide and wait to do horrible things to people. Rob them. Beat them. Even worse."

Jian Hyui felt his heart thumping against his chest. He thought it would surely burst through his flesh.

"I don't know what gang it was that did this. It doesn't matter. I never could understand what they did to people. I know now."

Jian Hyui stopped breathing.

"There were five of those awful thugs in the shadows. I never saw them until it was too late. They started following me. Talking sweetly to me. Making strange sounds. Whistling. But they scared me. I backed away and they surrounded me. They pushed me through an open doorway, into something like a tiny, filthy, smelly closet. They forced me to do awful things to them. Things I never imagined. They grabbed and touched me in places they shouldn't. Did things to me with their bodies. Held my face to parts of their filthy, stinking bodies that were disgusting. Then, one by one, they held my mouth closed so I couldn't scream as the others just watched. When they were finished with their pleasure they laughed and called me a slut and a pig. Then they all ran away back into the darkness. I have never been so frightened in my life."

Jian Hyui had tears streaming down his cheeks and he reached out to embrace her.

"No! Don't!" she screamed, backing away and holding up her hands as though in defense. "Don't *touch* me! I am shamed and I have shamed my family. My parents said it was *my* fault. Because I should not have disobeyed my fathers warning. I have dishonored my family. They became hysterical. That was the shouting you heard."

Meili's sobbing was uncontrollable and she clenched and unclenched her fists. She brushed away some of the long black hair that had fallen across her face and tried wiping away her tears. She was unraveling right in front of Jian. She paced like a frightened cat and then bolted for his door. She ran, not back toward her apartment, but for the stairwell that led to the rooftop. Jian ran after her, tripping over the hassock and stumbling before he reached his door. In a panic he tried to follow her up the dark, narrow spiral staircase and thrust open the heavy metal door to the rooftop. It was dark, but in the weak moonlight he saw Meili running toward the opposite side of the building. He frantically called her name.

A scream.

And then she was gone.

*Present day...*

Jian Hyui's own anguished scream awoke him from his restless sleep. His dreams were always the same. Always ended the same way. It wasn't a scream he had heard in his nightmare, but the loud singing of cicadas. He was standing on the edge of his building's rooftop, helplessly staring down at a beautiful, lifeless young body five stories below lying on the dusty, barren ground. And five young men dressed all in black stared back up at him...and pointed.

# 17

Jeremy Fleck lay wide-awake, flat on his back and staring at the ceiling in the dark bedroom of his father's house. He hadn't slept at all over the past two or three hours. A previously snoozing Beth Barnes at his side fluttered her eyes, rolled over and looked up at him.

"Your restlessness is disturbing my beauty sleep," she snickered.

"I'm sorry, my dear. Go back to sleep. It's nothing," Jeremy answered, trying to reassure *himself* as well as his beautiful friend.

"But you've been on edge for days now, I can sense it. Ever since you returned from Hong Kong," Beth responded with a concerned look on her face. "What is it?"

Jeremy Fleck let out a big sigh.

"I realize that I've been back here in London for only a couple of days. I returned too soon but I've got to return back home to Hong Kong again tomorrow. I have a sneaking suspicion that the authorities here have some concerns about my father's death. As does Devon Stone. I can sense it. Maybe I'm just being paranoid."

"Oh, go back to sleep, you big lummox," Beth said. "You have absolutely nothing to worry about. I don't understand your problem."

Jeremy wasn't so sure about that.

"I guess you're right," he answered with some lingering doubts. "I wish you could come with me this time. But soon. I promise."

"I'll miss you, Jeremy," Beth cooed, leaning in to give him a gentle kiss on his cheek. "Come back to London soon, my dear."

Within less than a minute she was snoozing once again.

Jeremy Fleck knew that his next course of action was to finally confront Jian Hyui face-to-face upon his return to Hong Kong. He should have done so following Hyui's amazing performance. But there was no way he could have gotten the privacy he required, and he was certain that Hyui surely would have panicked.

There was so much yet to be done here in London regarding his father's estate and he still had a job to contend with in Hong Kong. He was being pulled in different directions by his multiple responsibilities and his rattled mind wasn't helping the situation at all.

After spending a few more days visiting with Jian Hyui, and with Lydia playing tour guide to Devon, their flight back to London from Hong Kong had been delayed for several hours by stormy weather. When they finally landed, staggered bone-tired through customs, and headed out of Gatwick, Devon Stone and Lydia Hyui promptly fell asleep in the back of the taxicab. The dense fog in the area slowed traffic; such as it was at that hour, to a crawl. By the time the cabby awakened them in front of Devon's house it was nearly two-thirty A.M. Devon paid the cab driver and tipped him well. Probably better than he should have, but it was late and Devon was too bleary to fully pay attention.

Lydia was waiting at the top of the steps, leaning against the door and trying to keep her eyes open as Devon carried their small pieces of luggage up to the landing. He fumbled with his keys and thought he heard his telephone ringing inside.

"Bloody hell!" he exclaimed loudly making Lydia's eyes pop wide open. "Who has the unmitigated gall to be calling at *this* hour?"

He unlocked and then thrust open the door, making Lydia almost stumble in. He set their suitcases on the floor as he raced to get the telephone.

"Hello!" he practically screeched into the telephone. "So help me God, if this is a prank call or a wrong number I'll track you down and wring your bloody fucking neck!"

There was silence on the other end for a moment.

"I thought you didn't believe in God," said a female voice meekly.

Devon Stone hesitated for another moment. He recognized that voice. He motioned for Lydia to go on upstairs to bed.

"Veronica? Veronica Barron? Is that you?" he asked.

"Did I catch you at a bad time?" answered Veronica.

"Do you have any idea *what* time it is here, Miss Barron?" Devon said, beginning to calm down.

"Well, I've been trying to call you for days at various times and your phone just rings off the hook. Where the hell have you been? I thought someone might have murdered you."

"No, my dear," answered a groggy Devon Stone, fighting a yawn. "That only seems to happen when *you're* around."

"Ha! You and Billy think too much alike. Well, then, watch your back, Devon, because I'm headed back to London. My musical, *Nick and Nora,* is scheduled for a limited run on the West End and we begin rehearsals at the end of the week."

"Veronica, *please* let's discuss this at a reasonable hour. I've just gotten back from the Orient within the past hour and if I don't get to bed within the next three minutes you'll just be talking to dead air over here."

And so, at a reasonable hour the following afternoon, London time, Devon Stone and Veronica Barron discussed at great length her upcoming visit to London. He was elated that he would soon see his beautiful and talented young friend once again.

"I have a *splendid* idea, Veronica," Devon said after a sudden thought came to him. "If it's not too late to alter any plans you may have already made. I have no doubt that the producers of your show give you some sort of per diem for your accommodations, right? You say that it will be a limited run of…what? Three months? Tell your producers to save their money. Tell them to give you a bonus. Whatever. Instead of you booking a short lease on a boring flat or being put up in a stuffy hotel, as you well know I have five absolutely gorgeous bedrooms here at my place. Why not just stay *here* for the three-month run of your show? It might be fun."

Veronica Barron was taken aback and thought about it for a few seconds.

"Wow, that is *awfully* generous of you, Devon. Are you sure?"

"I wouldn't have offered it if I thought otherwise. But if by any chance the run of your show is extended we can make adjustments. I can take house guests for only so long."

They both laughed.

"You know that Billy will fly over just before opening night…and probably stay a few days before and afterwards. Will that be okay with you?"

"Don't be silly, my dear. Of course it's perfectly okay. I'll just go ahead and soundproof your room so I won't be able to hear any embarrassing wild lovemaking squeals going on."

"Well… Billy *can* be loud at times," Veronica answered.

"Stop it, Veronica! I was being facetious."

"Oh," was her somewhat embarrassed simple reply, followed by a giggle.

"And put your Billy Bennett at ease, while you're at it. You'll be perfectly safe from any of my rakish charms. I certainly won't be trying any shenanigans while you're here. I have been seeing someone since you and I last spoke. I think the two of you will get on fabulously. She's a very interesting young lady."

"*How* young, Devon?"

"Let's just say that she's younger than I am and just slightly older than you are."

"Ahhh, huh. I see, then. Is *your* bedroom soundproofed?"

Early the following week, Veronica Barron arrived at the home of Devon stone. And then the following day, seven large trunks of clothing arrived as well.

Devon took one look at the trunks as they were being carried into the house by the airline's delivery service.

"Bloody hell," he said, turning to Veronica. "Did you buy out Bergdorf-Goodman before you left home? I just may have to give you *two* of my bedrooms for all of your…stuff. Will there be any more coming over or is this it?"

She waved him off as she started to carry one of the smaller trunks upstairs.

"Nah, this is it. For now. I may have to go out to Harrods for a bit more as the weeks go by, though."

He rolled his eyes as he lifted another one of the trunks and followed her up the stairs.

"Where's your lady friend?" Veronica asked.

"Lydia is at her bookshop at the moment," he answered. "She may or may not stop by later. I have no idea what her schedule is today. She doesn't stay here with me all the time. Only occasionally. She's a very pleasant distraction, to say the least."

Veronica stopped, put the trunk down and put her hands on her hips.

"I'm *certainly* sure she wouldn't want to be called a distraction, Devon. Pleasant or otherwise."

*Well, there you go,* Devon thought. *Veronica being Veronica as only she can.*

"That may have been a poor choice of words on my part, Veronica, but my publisher keeps hounding me about my next book. I find that my mind is anywhere but on my next murder when she's around."

"Have you been keeping yourself out of harm's way since I saw you last, Devon? You seem to attract danger."

Devon Stone laughed.

"Only when you're around, my dear. Only when you're around."

At that precise moment, Jeremy Fleck, white-knuckled, gripped the armrests of his seat as the airplane made that final dramatic turn heading to Hong Kong's Kai-Tak runway in the harbor. He felt his ears pop as the airplane made its rapid drop. The stormy weather had made the approach to the airport even more frightening with sudden turbulence drawing gasps from his fellow passengers as the craft dipped, dropped and then steadied itself once again.

As many times as he had flown into and out of Kai Tak, he had never been able to quell the nervousness and often wondered why there hadn't been onboard heart attacks from faint of heart passengers.

Jeremy Fleck breathed a sigh of relief as he heard and felt the tires make contact with the runway, even as the rainwater still flowed horizontally outside his window. He had to chuckle, though, as several of his fellow passengers applauded. Grateful for a safe arrival, no doubt.

He made a mad dash from the airport to his office to wrap up some unfinished business and to return a few long neglected telephone calls. Then that was followed by a return to his apartment to change his clothes and collect his thoughts.

He was tired from the long flight and thought about what his next course of action might be. He brewed a pot of tea and, carrying a steaming cup, he strolled over to the window and stared out across the harbor. His apartment was on the tenth floor of a high-rise overlooking Victoria Harbour. He was able to see the airport runways and watched as two Star ferries passed each other between Kowloon and Hong Kong Island. The rain was easing up and there were a few breaks in the clouds overhead.

His thoughts bouncing back and forth between two incessant concerns, Jeremy was fairly certain that Jian Hyui wouldn't have mentioned to his sister about that deadly incident on one of those ferries but he did *not* know to what extent Hyui had mentioned his friendship with Samuel Fleck. Lydia Hyui and Devon Stone had been pleasant enough at the memorial, but Jeremy had picked up a vibe that told him Devon was skeptical about his father's suicide. And that concerned him deeply.

First things first.

He would have to be cautious in his next approach to Jian Hyui. The man was neither as innocent nor as harmless as he appeared.

# 18

He tried to resist going back into Kowloon Walled City, but Jian Hyui seemed emboldened for some reason. There had been a steady rain pouring for most of the day and, initially, he thought that would thwart any plans he may have had. But the rain had eased and there had been a beautiful sunset.

He donned his usual attire and collected the two long knives that Lau had, indeed, presented to him as his own following the rapturous success of the opera.

It was dark and very wet as he slowly made his way through the narrow alleyways of this hellish place. The corridor through which he walked was barely wide enough for two to walk abreast.

Suddenly, a few hundred feet in front of him a huge, lumbering figure dressed entirely in black appeared from the shadows. The figure was tall and almost as wide as the alleyway itself. Hyui froze in his tracks when he saw the frightening silhouette and decided then and there to make a hasty retreat.

Too late.

The man hadn't really planned on a robbery this evening, but he saw what he thought was a little old lady turning away from him. *Easy cash* he thought as he chuckled and started running toward his victim.

Jian thought he would make it back to safety when all of a sudden he was grabbed from behind.

"Not so fast, little lady," hissed the attacker leaning close to Jian's ear. Jian recoiled from the foul smelling breath of his attacker. "Don't be afraid," the man continued as he let out a maniacal laugh. He had a firm grip on Jian's collar.

He spun Jian Hyui around and was shocked to make an unexpected discovery.

"What the…? Well, what do we have here? What the *fuck* are you, some kinda queer or something?"

Jian Hyui resisted and managed to get free of the man's grasp. But the large man pulled out a switchblade knife and Jian heard it click open.

"Don't worry, sweetie, just hand over your purse and, surprise, surprise, if you don't faint or piss in your panties you can run along home."

But the attacker was the one in for a surprise.

Jian backed away, as if to run away. The attacker swung out with his switchblade but Jian Hyui ducked. The man slipped on the slick, wet pavement losing his balance.

As Jian ducked, he swiftly pulled the long knives from his garments and thrust upwards. And it was an amazingly forceful thrust.

Speed and surprise. Actually it was something that neither man was expecting at the moment.

One blade went straight up through the underside of the attacker's chin, up into his mouth, slicing through the man's tongue and into the roof of his mouth before piercing the nasal passages. Hyui's second blade swiftly swept across the man's throat, rupturing the windpipe causing what one might call a significant respiratory compromise. This even surprised Jian Hyui who stood back and listened to the rasping gurgling sounds of the man trying to breathe. The shocked man tried to scream because of the excruciating pain but his mouth couldn't open because of the position of the blade lodged in his skull.

The fact that the evil man was still alive, although just barely, stunned Hyui as he reached out, trying to dislodge his blade from the attacker's jaw but it wouldn't budge.

Gasping desperately for breath and without thinking, the man reached up with both hands grabbing Jian's blade trying to pull it free from his face but he sliced his fingers practically to the bone on the knife and his blood flowed freely down his arms. Finally, from lack of oxygen both to his lungs and to his brain, the man looked at Jian with fury in his eyes and was, in effect, dead before he even hit the wet, slippery pavement. His brief death rattle sent shivers down Hyui's spine.

Jian Hyui stood there in shock staring at the dead hulk lying there at his feet. He had to do something before any more people decided to walk down this particular pathway. Blood was spreading around his feet as he reached down and grabbed the handle of the knife protruding from the man's chin.

He put his foot on the corpse to give him leverage and pulled as hard as he could but it still didn't move.

He heard laughing and voices approaching through a dark alleyway that emptied into the area where he now stood. Panic rose in his mind and his heart started racing.

He was *not* going to leave his precious knife and flee.

He mustered all the strength he could find within him, twisted and yanked on the handle once again.

He heard a crack of bone and cartilage.

The blade came free along with a couple teeth and some bone fragments.

He grabbed his knife, concealed it along with the other in his garments and hastily disappeared into the shadows.

He was still running when he heard a woman's piercing scream coming from the long alleyway he had just left.

He ran a little faster until the dark swallowed him up, leaving the fetid aroma of death behind him.

# 19

The tantalizing aromas wafting through Devon Stone's house were precursors to the sumptuous meal ahead. The talented author was also considered an unapologetic epicurean to all of his friends. He entertained often, serving his many guests anything from lavish several-course meals to simple buffets and brunches. Sometimes he would hire cooks, bartenders, and serving staff, depending upon the number of guests attending; other times he, himself, did all the food preparation. He came by it naturally and had been taught well. Devon Stone was the pen name for Daniel Stein, also his father's name. Both of his parents were professional chefs and had owned Danny's Steak House, a once popular, long since shuttered restaurant in SoHo. The young Devon, nee Daniel, often helped in the hustling, bustling restaurant both in the kitchen and the dining room, eventually turning that experience into the subject matter for his first best-selling thriller, *A Taste For Murder*. He had lost his virginity at the tender age of fifteen to a saucy sous-chef named Amalia, ten years his senior. He worked *that* titillating episode into his first thriller as well.

Veronica Barron had arrived from the U.S. two days before in preparation for the rehearsals of her musical *Nick & Nora* opening on the West End a few short weeks away.

As a welcome dinner, Devon was preparing one of his favorites. It was time consuming, but worth it. Beginning with an appetizer of a prawn cocktail, the main meal would consist of Beef Wellington, Yorkshire pudding, and glazed carrots. Lydia Hyui was preparing a simple, classic Chinese salad with chopped spring onions, sliced radishes, blanched spinach, and chopped tender lotus stem.

Veronica and Lydia, having been introduced the night before, chatted side by side in the kitchen, as the salad was being prepared.

"Okay, folks," Devon announced, clapping his hands together. "It's cocktail time. Our other guests have finally arrived. Dinner will be ready in about thirty minutes or so…if we're lucky. Let's try to get soused first, shall we?"

The trio headed down the hall to the parlor off of the main entryway. Veronica got a huge smile on her face when she recognized the handsome, elderly man standing there. He handed a wrapped dish to Devon and both men smiled. Devon took the dish and headed to the kitchen. He hurried right back.

"Chester!" she said loudly. "Oh, my goodness. How great to see you again!"

Chester Davenport was Devon's longtime friend and neighbor. He was also the retired Director of MI6.

Chester and Veronica hugged each other and Veronica planted a sweet kiss on his cheek. Veronica hadn't even noticed that another woman had been standing right behind Chester. The tall, slender woman, with shockingly white, close-cropped hair was elegantly attired in a form fitting long black skirt, an emerald green sleek silk blouse and with a striking, attention-getting dark green Malachite necklace which Veronica immediately fell in love with. Although she was nearing seventy, she looked much younger. She winked at Devon as she watched Veronica kiss her date.

"Veronica," said Chester Davenport, "Devon and Lydia already know this young lady," as he turned to his date, "but let me introduce *you* to the infamous Fiona Thayer."

Oh", Veronica responded, with a hand to her mouth, "I'm so sorry. I was so excited to see Chester that I was oblivious. That was so rude of me."

Veronica kept staring at that gorgeous necklace…and with the earrings to match.

"Oh, bosh!" laughed Fiona Thayer, "don't be silly. I've heard all about your exploits and Chester's involvement. It's a distinct pleasure meeting you, my dear."

And Fiona reached out her hand to Veronica.

"By the by, I loved you in *Private Lives* a few years ago and I, for one, am eager to see your new show. Neither of these gents here cares for musicals, I understand."

"Drinks, everyone...drinks!" interjected a slightly embarrassed Devon Stone. "Let's get this party started, shall we?"

Forty-five minutes later, with drinks downed and enjoyed, the group seated themselves at the elegantly laid out dining room table. The chatter and laughter continued as they immediately started eating the prawn cocktails.

"Fiona," began Veronica, "I should have asked while we were all drinking, but what did Chester mean when he introduced you earlier as the *infamous* Fiona Thayer? Was he being facetious? Should I perhaps have heard of you in some way? Are you, too, in the theater or films over here? I'm sorry, but your name is unfamiliar to me."

Fiona chuckled.

"Please let me explain, my dear," interrupted Chester Davenport, as he placed a gentle hand on Fiona's shoulder.

There was silence for a moment. Fiona gave Chester a warm smile and a nod.

The prawns finished, platters of food were being passed around as Chester began to speak.

"When we first met, Veronica, you and your two American friends had gotten yourselves into a bit of a...well...shall we say, tangle with some nasty people."

Veronica Barron remembered only too well.

"My good friend Fiona, here, had been involved well before you arrived on the scene."

"Oh, cut to the chase, Chester," Fiona laughed, waving him off. "I'm an assassin, dear. Plain and simple."

Veronica sat agape.

"I was one of Devon's group of friends targeting those murdering

Nazi sympathizers before you and your friends arrived on the scene and got involved. But I had been shot, stabbed and nearly strangled. I was not expected to live. I sure as hell fooled *them*, didn't I?" And she laughed raucously. "That's why I said earlier that I heard about *your* exploits. You sure are a gutsy gal yourself, aren't you, dear?"

"Close your mouth, Veronica," said Devon Stone chuckling. "I can see your tonsils."

Veronica stared at this elegant, seemingly refined lady sitting across the table from her.

"An...assassin. Ahh...can I assume that that's *not* your day job, or whatever?"

Fiona, Chester and Devon howled. Lydia Hyui chuckled.

"Well, my dear, I certainly don't have that on my résumé, so to speak. But it's in my dossier."

"Now *I'll* cut to the chase, Veronica," snickered Devon. "Sweet Fiona here, although now retired and long since out of the game, was one of MI6's better spies. Incognito, of course. One of the rare few *female* spies, at that. No, of course you wouldn't have been familiar with her name. She went by several, by the way. She also worked in conjunction with MI5 here at home. Although it's long after the fact, and we shouldn't really be discussing this, she was part of the 5th-column operations, ferreting out Nazi sympathizers here in London. Let's just say that she has several notches on her gunstock and leave it at that. Metaphorically speaking that is."

Fiona Thayer and Devon Stone exchanged winks.

"Ah, but *now* that you know this wicked little secret, Veronica," Chester Davenport said, shaking his head, looking serious and shrugging his shoulders, "we'll have to kill you."

Loud laughter all around the table. Well, except from Veronica.

"Relax, dear," Fiona laughingly said to Veronica, shaking *her* head. "Relax. It's an old spy joke. Old, lame, and not very funny."

The group continued eating in silence for a few minutes.

"Delicious, Devon, simply divine," Fiona said after a bite of the beef.

"While we're on the subject of murder, Devon..." began Chester.

Devon Stone froze, shook his head slightly toward his friend as if saying "don't go there" but it was too late. He closed his eyes. And waited.

"Are you still toying with the thought that your friend Fleck was murdered?"

The fork full of glazed carrots that was headed towards Veronica's mouth stopped in mid-journey. It was so-noted by Devon. He quickly tried to change the subject.

"Save room for dessert, friends, Chester brought another one of his creations for us!"

Devon Stone had cannabis growing in his basement, aided by warming, glowing grow lights. Chester Davenport harvested some of the herb on occasion and infused it in his many baking projects.

"Are they your wonderful brownies?" asked Veronica, remembering them from a few years ago. "They were *so* good!"

"Oh, no, Veronica," answered Davenport, "Devon told me what he was planning on preparing for dinner, so we needed something a bit more elegant to compliment this fabulous meal. I experimented with an old cheesecake recipe I've had for years and came up with a delicacy that was on that plate I handed to Devon as we entered this evening. The secret is in the crust." And he winked.

"To *die* for!" exclaimed a smiling Fiona Thayer, putting a hand on Chester's shoulder.

*Wrong choice of words* thought Devon Stone.

It looked as though Veronica was about to say something.

Devon cleared his throat.

"I recognize that look, Miss Barron...or perhaps now I should say Mrs. Bennett. I remember it well and also remember where it has led us in the not too distant past."

Veronica Barron Bennett sat back in her chair, folded her hands on her lap and gave Devon *the* stare.

"Before you go wandering too far off base," he continued, "the situation to which dear Chester here alluded was a suicide, not a murder."

"But..." interrupted Chester Davenport, and Devon shot up his hand, palm out, as if to silence his friend.

"It has been classified as a suicide. As far as I know, that's where it stands. That was several months ago. It may or may not still be under investigation. I have *nothing* to do with it aside from the fact that the poor bloke was a fellow author and a friend of mine."

Lydia Hyui sat back and remained silent, although she knew that Devon thought something about the situation didn't seem to make sense. But she would let Devon take the lead.

"Oh," was all that Veronica said as she resumed eating.

"But just think, dear," said Fiona Thayer with a smile, "you'll get to solve a murder…or murders every night on stage!"

Devon Stone and Lydia Hyui glanced at each other and Devon winked.

"Who's ready for some cheesecake?" he asked.

Several hours later the after-dinner drinks had been downed, Chester and Fiona had said their goodbyes, the pots, pans, and dishes had been done and put away, and Veronica and Lydia had retired to their respective bedrooms. Devon made sure his front door was locked and he turned out all the lights. As he climbed the stairs he thought about Samuel Fleck once again. He was hoping to get some answers but he knew that hope was not a strategy.

He just didn't know what his strategy should be.

Veronica Barron would be off-book when her first rehearsal began the following afternoon. Even the slight rewrite for her part, Nora Charles, here in the London production was imbedded in her mind and she was ready to go. Every word memorized.

A new eleven o'clock number had been written for her, better than the one she sang in the Broadway production, and she knew that she would nail it. Every note, every lyric memorized.

She thought about the young baritone who would be revealed as the killer as the show came to a thrilling climax. He was *way* too suave and handsome to be a killer, wasn't he? And she muffled a giggle. The New York audiences always seemed to be surprised when they found out "who dunnit". The critics, in their reviews, had offered no spoilers.

But all of these thoughts were not why Veronica Barron lay awake and staring at the ceiling at three-thirty A.M.

No, she was thinking about something else.

One subject had been mentioned, and then abruptly shunted away from, at the dinner the previous evening.

The subject was murder.

Veronica Barron's curiosity was piqued.

Suddenly, in the bedroom one floor directly above hers, Devon Stone's eyes popped open. It had been a restless sleep as it was, and he was concerned that he might disturb Lydia who seemed to be sleeping soundly beside him. He had been thinking about Veronica's propensity for...well, for sticking her cute little nose into business she should *not* be sticking her cute little nose into. He saw the look on her face when Chester Davenport mentioned the questionable suicide of Samuel Fleck. He had seen that very look on more occasions than he would like. And she had gotten herself involved in more occasions than he would like. Actually, it was associative interference. And it had come with associative dangers. *But.* And here was the big "but". She had a show to prepare for and in which to perform. She certainly did not need any distractions. *He* did not need any distractions. He had a book to write and an impatient publisher practically breathing down his neck. Too many thoughts were swirling around in his head. Veronica. Murder. Suicide. Book. Suicide. Murder.

*Fuck!* Devon thought to himself as he rolled over and tried to get back to sleep.

Billy Bennett was due to arrive shortly before Veronica's opening night. Perhaps that, and the show itself, would be all the distractions that Veronica needed.

Before he realized it, soft morning light slowly crept through the partially opened drapes in his bedroom.

And he had not been able to fall back to sleep.

# 20

Two hours later, Lydia Hyui was in the kitchen frying bacon and scrambling eggs while the coffee pot perked loudly on the counter. She expected that the salivating-inducing aromas drifting up the stairway would entice both Devon and his houseguest and they would soon be joining her. When she heard a slight rustling noise behind her, she turned. At first she was startled. She blinked her eyes. And then she laughed uncontrollably.

Devon Stone was standing there, unshaven stubble, ruddy-faced, dark circles under his eyes, disheveled hair sticking out in every possible direction, rumpled unbuttoned pajamas protruding from a barely tied dressing gown and a look of confusion on his face.

"What the hell are you laughing at, Lydia?" he asked as he leaned up against the door jamb.

"Well, for one thing, Devon, you look as though you've just barely survived electrocution."

He stood there just staring at her for a brief second, and then ambled over to the refrigerator as if in a daze. He opened it and peered inside, looking up and down on each shelf.

"Any of that cheesecake left?" he asked.

Eight hours earlier, local time, Jian Hyui stood in silent thought, leaning on a railing as the Star Ferry made its way from Kowloon Peninsula to Hong Kong Island. A new opera was in rehearsal and, although he wasn't a lead character this time, Hyui looked forward to performing once again. It wouldn't be nearly as strenuous as his role as Mulan. In fact, it wouldn't be strenuous at all. It would simply be fun. The late morning sun felt warm on his back as the boat sailed swiftly across the calm water. A large nesting area for black kites was on the east side of Victoria Peak and Hyui watched as one of these large birds of prey rode the air currents above, then swiftly swooped down to snatch a dead fish that had been floating on the harbor waters. The kites were more scavengers than hunters and attackers.

His thoughts now were about Kowloon Walled City, and *other* attackers. He was ready mentally and prepared weapon-wise for another journey through its dark, dank alleyways. Nightfall couldn't come soon enough. In his mind, he was swinging and slashing his treasured blades across the neck of one of the Triads.

At that precise moment, and completely by coincidence, someone tapped him on the shoulder making him jump.

He let out a frightened little yelp as he spun around.

"Dǎrǎo yīxià?" *Excuse me?* Hyui asked, wide-eyed, as he stood face-to-face with the mysterious Caucasian man who had caused the panic on the ferry weeks before.

"I think it's time you and I had a little chat, Jian," said the man, as he seemed to step closer.

If it weren't for the fact that he couldn't swim, Jian Hyui in that instant considered leaping overboard.

An uncharacteristically clear morning in London sent rays of brilliant sunshine streaming in through the kitchen windows as a perky Veronica Barron practically bounced into the room.

"Good morning, you two," she said cheerily, "Isn't this a *glorious* day?"

She suddenly took a look at Devon.

"Oh, my…Devon, what's the matter? You look…well, ah…oh, wow, what's the matter?"

Lydia Hyui stifled a snicker and picked some bacon out of the skillet with a pair of tongs and placed it onto a platter.

"Jesus, bloody hell, I certainly don't look *that* bad. Do I?"

Veronica and Lydia looked at one another, and then turned in Devon's direction both of them nodding their heads in unison.

"Oh, fuck off," he said as he turned and stomped out of the kitchen.

The two women turned to look at each other once again. And they laughed so hard tears were streaming down their cheeks.

Two minutes later Devon Stone slowly walked back into the kitchen. He had flattened down his unruly hair, and had tightened the dressing gown belt around his waist.

"Well, that's a bit better," chuckled Veronica. "At least now you're smiling."

Devon's brow furrowed slightly.

"Am I? Actually it's purely unintentional."

"I'm sorry," said Jeremy Fleck, "I really didn't mean to frighten you, Jian."

Frightened was too tame a word. Jian Hyui was terrified at this precise moment. And he looked it.

"I realize you might be thinking that your life is in danger right now because of me, but I assure you, that couldn't be further from the truth."

Jian Hyui regretted that he didn't have those two long knives with him now. Not that he would attempt to try to use them here, on board, in broad daylight, in the middle of Victoria Harbour. But they would be... or *could* be protection if needed.

"In one respect, I want to thank you for making my father happy in your own little way."

Jian Hyui was confused. *What the hell was this man talking about? And who the hell is he? And how the hell does he know my name?* Hyui thought.

"I've known about you for some time now, young man. I know that your life *had* been in danger. In *serious* danger. That's why I acted the way I did and intervened."

Jian shook his head, trying to decipher what was going on. Was he hallucinating?

"Do you have me confused with someone else?" he asked. "I've seen you twice and you've confounded me and frightened me both times. But I have no idea who you are and why you seem to be following me. Is it because of something I've done in Kowloon Walled City? Are you connected to the law?"

Now Jeremy Fleck laughed.

"No, I'm certainly *not* connected to the law, Jian, although I think I have a pretty good idea what you have done in that horrid place. I don't know *why*, though. That's not my concern at the moment, however. But I definitely have *not* confused you with someone else. I'm Jeremy Fleck. Samuel Fleck's son."

Jian Hyui felt that he might pass out. He was suddenly lightheaded. Jeremy Fleck caught him as his knees buckled.

"I apologize, ladies," Devon said as he headed toward the coffee pot, empty cup in hand. "That was very rude of me. After I glanced at my pitiful reflection in a mirror I realized why you both reacted the way you did. I had a fitful sleep last night and I guess it took a toll on my normally unbelievably handsome face."

"Let's *not* get carried away," Veronica laughed. "I, too, laid awake for a while last night, Devon, but look, I'm still a ravishing beauty." She tossed back her long blonde hair first with one hand and then the other.

Lydia Hyui stared at the both of them, shaking her head.

"Well, take a seat Prince Charming and Rapunzel, breakfast is ready."

Although he was visibly shaken, Jian Hyui and Jeremy Fleck took a seat side by side on an unoccupied bench in the middle of the vessel's deck.

By the time the ferry pulled into the pier on Hong Kong Island a few minutes later, Jeremy Fleck had rapidly covered a lot of territory regarding his relationship with his father and why he had been following Hyui.

Regarding his father's suicide? Jeremy Fleck said that he was still too emotional about it to discuss it in any detail. Jian Hyui found that unusual, but didn't pursue the issue. But he was sure to question his sister about it to find out what she and Devon Stone might know.

Hyui sat back and looked off, not really focusing on anything in particular. The apprehension he had felt moments ago slowly dissipated, segueing into more confusion than anything else. He knew, now, that Jeremy Fleck was a murderer. He had just confessed to that crime that had taken place several weeks earlier right here, possibly on this very vessel. But did Jeremy Fleck know that *he*, Jian Hyui, was *also* a murderer of a few of the notorious Triad gang members? Fleck seemed to *imply* that he did. But then, maybe he was just guessing.

*We are each playing roles*, Jian Hyui thought. *But are we the victims or the villains?*

Jeremy Fleck stared out across the harbor and Jian Hyui stared at Jeremy Fleck.

"You are more handsome than your father," Jian Hyui finally said wistfully. "Was he jealous of you?"

Jeremy chuckled.

"In one respect, yes, I guess he was jealous," answered Jeremy, "but not for my looks. And, in another respect, I think he may have feared me. Feared me for what I might divulge."

"You mean," Jian Hyui asked, "about his perverted sexuality?"

"Oh, good grief, no," laughed Jeremy. "Not at all. That was not as well kept a secret as he thought. No, no. There was something else he and I both were keeping secret."

*Indeed*, thought Jian Hyui once again, *we are each playing a role, aren't we?*

"Will Don Ameche still be playing Nick Charles over here?" asked Lydia Hyui.

"No, unfortunately," answered Veronica. "He was committed to a film role and couldn't break the contract. Too bad, because I thought he was perfect."

"So who will be your new costar?" asked Devon.

"Our producers tried like the devil to get Rex Harrison, but he's involved in something else and was unavailable."

"*Rex Harrison?*" asked an astonished Lydia. "He's handsome as all get-out, but I didn't know *he* could sing."

"Well, I seriously doubt that he can, from what I've heard", answered Veronica with a chuckle. "That's why this thing he's involved with will probably flop, sorry to say. Evidently it's a musical version of *Pygmalion*. It hasn't started rehearsals yet, though. Probably will close out of town and he'll wish he had taken the part alongside me over here. Doesn't sound all that interesting, if you ask me. A musical about teaching someone how to speak proper English? Seriously? Frankly, it could be a career-killer."

Veronica took a slight pause, and then had a quizzical look on her face.

"Huh, now that I mention killer…"

Devon Stone was raising a cup of coffee to his lips and it stopped halfway. He closed his eyes, hoping that a dreaded question wouldn't be coming next.

It was. And it did.

"Why did you steer so abruptly away from Chester's question last evening about your friend's suicide, Devon?"

Devon took a deep breath and thought about how to phrase an answer that would be appropriate, not be too harsh…but one that would dissuade Veronica from pursuing the topic any further.

"Please don't give it a second thought, my dear," he answered. "You need to concentrate on your show. Seriously. Chester was taking a flippant comment I had made out of context. I joked…and, yes, it was in *very* poor taste…that perhaps Fleck *didn't* commit suicide, but was killed by one of his loyal, faithful readers because of his last dreadful book. That's all. Nothing more than that."

Lydia Hyui knew that Devon Stone was honest to the bone, but she also knew that he had just lied.

Veronica Barron knew that Devon Stone probably just lied.

Devon Stone knew that Lydia Hyui knew that he had just lied. He wasn't so sure about Veronica.

Silence in the kitchen.

"So, then," Devon began, hoping to break the uncomfortable silence and change the subject. "Who's your new leading man going to be?"

"Well, he almost looks the part as well as Don Ameche did, and he's in between movies so his run, too, is very limited. He's charming enough, though. And we really do seem to have great chemistry on stage. David Niven."

106

"Oh," perked up Lydia. "Wasn't he in that racy film last year with William Holden? What was it...*The Moon Is Blue*?"

"That's the one," answered Veronica. "I'm hoping that we can make it work. He seems to be struggling just a bit with a passable American accent, but it's coming along by the day. His comic timing is wonderful. He's very funny, though, and has a decent enough singing voice, but the little dog playing Asta growls at him all the time."

"Tell him to rub a nice raw filet mignon on his face before they have scenes together," Devon chuckled. "The audiences will *love* what that dog does then!"

# 21

*Remember, remember, the 5th of November…*

Ever since 1605 the British have been celebrating the 5th of November much the same way those in the U.S.A. celebrate the 4th of July. Bonfire Night, or Guy Fawkes Night commemorates the failed attempt of Fawkes and his coconspirators to blow up the Houses of Parliament while the King was inside.

Bonfires are set ablaze throughout the country along with effigies of Guy Fawkes, which are then burned on the fires. For days leading up to the big night, children roam through the streets pulling wagons with an effigy sitting within and calling "Penny for the Guy". They are begging for coins so they may go and purchase firecrackers to shoot off during the celebrations. The Guy is usually made of old clothes stuffed with straw or newspaper. Abundant firework displays and firecrackers of all types and sizes are shot off for hours on end, spooking cattle, causing howling dogs to cower in secluded corners and making cats go into hiding for several days afterwards.

*…Gunpowder, treason and plot.*
*I see no reason*
*Why gunpowder treason*
*Should ever be forgot.*

Billy Bennett remembered Bonfire Night well. The fun part, before the scary part when his friend, Peyton Chase, was shot.

Devon Stone remembered Bonfire Night as one, three years earlier, where a local murderous Nazi sympathizer was caught, tormented, and dispatched by one of Devon's group of friends, never to be seen or heard from again.

It had been three years since Billy had been back in London and when he found out that the opening night to Veronica's show would be on Thursday, November 11th, he was ecstatic. He had been like a little kid that night back then, setting off firecrackers all up and down street after street. He was hoping, that when he got back to London, he would be able to locate the same, practically toothless, old guy who sold him the pyrotechnics back then.

He and Veronica had been on the telephone longer than originally planned, but they had a lot of catching up to do. It was the longest they had been apart since getting married.

"Hey, cowboy," Veronica finally said, after glancing at her watch, "I gotta run. I'll be late for rehearsal and they've written yet *another* whole new song for today. Kisses, kisses, kisses…I love you and goodbye!"

The call ended before Billy could even say another word.

She was rushing down the stairs and Devon called out to her.

"I forgot to ask, Veronica, in which theater will your show be playing?"

"We'll be playing at the Savoy this time," Veronica said, as she hurriedly rushed to head out to rehearsal.

"Wonderful old theater," Devon acknowledged. "I've seen many excellent shows there. My favorite being *Blithe Spirit*, back in '41. Did you know that in 1881 it became the very first public building in the world to be lit entirely by electricity?"

"I'm not even going to give you the pleasure of asking how you know that, Devon," Veronica snickered.

Devon Stone laughed loudly, clapping his hands. "How are rehearsals going, by the way?"

"Okay, I guess," answered Veronica shrugging her shoulders. "The actress playing one of the murder victims frightens me however."

"In what way?"

"Well, when she sings she sounds like Minnie Mouse imitating Ethel Merman."

Devon Stone simply stared at her.

"And just how does *that* frighten you?"

"She's hilarious, Devon, absolutely *hilarious*. Her comic timing is priceless. I fear that *she'll* be getting more laughs than *I* will."

"Ahh, the fragile ego of the diva," answered Devon with a wink. "Fortunately us writers don't have such egos."

Veronica put her hands on her hips.

"Oh, stuff it! Really, smartass?" she said glowering at him. "Don't tell me *your* ego isn't shattered when *you* get bad reviews."

"Frankly my dear, I wouldn't know about that," he responded with a haughty air and a shrug of his shoulders. "Haven't experienced that yet."

Veronica just rolled her eyes.

"Liar!" she laughingly shouted as she hustled out the front door.

Devon Stone chuckled to himself as he remembered a quote from Oscar Levant.

*What the world needs is more geniuses with humility; there are so few of us left.*

Jian Hyui didn't have any reason to *not* believe what Jeremy Fleck had told him, but he had the feeling that the man had not been totally forthcoming regarding the suicide. Perhaps he had read too many of Devon Stone's mysteries, but something about Fleck's tale didn't seem to ring true.

Jeremy Fleck had told Jian about his father's despondency over his last three books but hadn't gone into any further detail. Not wanting to offend any of Jian's sensitive feelings, Jeremy Fleck had treaded very carefully when he discussed his father's many indiscretions over the years... with both genders. Jeremy had carefully monitored his father's activities whenever he visited Hong Kong. Samuel Fleck never knew that his son was doing so. Jeremy was *as* discrete as his father was *not*.

Jian Hyui was stunned when Jeremy told him about the man who had been shot on the Star Ferry that horrendous morning months ago. Known only to him as Qiang, Jian knew that he was a member of one of the notorious Triads. He had encountered Qiang once, while he was wandering innocently through Kowloon Walled City pretending to check out the various shops. Jian, of course, was actually there for *another* reason: to plot out his course for possible future revenge. At that time, he just didn't know how he might go about doing it. Without watching where he was walking, Jian bumped into Qiang and had apologized profusely. For some reason the awful man had taken an instant liking to the gentle Jian Hyui and, while obviously concealing his true disposition from the rest of his gang members, propositioned him. Jian was aghast. The man was ugly. The man was frightening. The man's body odor was sickening. Jian backed away, but Qiang followed him, laughing. Qiang didn't take rejection well. He persisted. And would often follow Jian heckling him. And threatening him.

But how did Jeremy Fleck know all this?

# 22

Billy Bennett arrived at Devon Stone's house with a lot of flair and very little luggage. Dapper as always, wearing a hunter green nubby tweed sport coat, open-collared white button-down shirt, tan corduroy slacks and a stylish trilby hat sitting rakishly at an angle on his handsome head, he paid and tipped the taxicab driver, grabbed his suitcase and jogged up the front steps.

Before he reached the top step another cab pulled up in front of the house. Veronica Barron leaped from the car, bounding up the stairs where she met Billy in an extremely warm embrace, knocking Billy's hat off in the process. They were kissing *very* passionately as Devon threw open his front door.

"Jesus Christ, get your arses in here before you get her pregnant out there on the steps. This is a respectable neighborhood. Or was," he called down to them.

They both ran up the stairs toward the open door. Veronica ran past him and on into the house.

Devon quickly placed his hand on Billy's chest, preventing him from entering.

"What?" asked Billy, with a confused look on his face.

Devon Stone nodded back down toward the steps. Billy turned and looked.

"Oh," he said as he, too, chuckled.

He went back down the stairs halfway to retrieve his hat. Then went all the way back down to pay Veronica's awaiting, laughing cabbie.

*I may regret not having that bedroom soundproofed* Devon thought to himself as he slowly closed the front door after Billy had come inside. He shook his head and rolled his eyes.

An hour later the trio was enjoying a platter of various sliced cheeses and cold meats accompanied by crispy, wafer-thin crackers.

"So, may I assume, then, that your buddy Peyton is watching the store while you're gone, right?" asked Devon as he handed a scotch on the rocks to Billy. "Cheers, by the way, and here's to your safe arrival and to Veronica's play," Devon continued, hoisting his own gin and tonic.

"No, actually," Billy Bennett answered, "as luck or fate would have it, Peyton headed over to this side of the pond practically at the same time I did. Something about Anoushka being in Paris for some reason and we left the shop in the very capable hands of his father and the very contemptible hands of his cousin, Karen. They didn't kill each other last time, so we figure all is good."

Veronica snickered.

"I've met cousin Karen a few times," she said. "Peyton's dad needs a Purple Heart simply for putting up with the harridan. To say that she's sarcastic is putting it mildly."

Billy laughed, shaking his head. "You might want to add the word snarky, as well. Maybe even bitchy."

"Be nice, Billy," Veronica said with a wry smile. "And let's be fair. She's actually become much nicer since she started dating the Turtle."

Devon looked at her quizzically.

"Hold on a minute. Did I misunderstand? Peyton's cousin is dating a…turtle?" he asked incredulously.

Billy Bennett guffawed.

"Tuttle, actually," Billy answered. "His name is Franklin Tuttle. But we all call him the Turtle because he hasn't ever wanted to stray too far away from home."

Devon Stone just stared and furrowed his brow.

"Oh. Well," Billy said when he saw the look on Devon's face. "Maybe you might *not* know this, but box turtles, which he sorta resembles, rarely ever roam more than a mile or so from where they were hatched. It really stresses them out if they are moved from their environment."

"Actually, I did *not* know that, Billy," Devon said, shaking his head as he went to fix another gin and tonic. *Americans are a weird lot*, Devon thought to himself, still shaking his head.

"In any event," Billy said, "getting back to Peyton, I sure hope he gets to relax and enjoy himself over here...well, in Paris, I mean. He'll probably stop off here in London to catch Ronnie's show before he heads home. If he's still able to walk, that is, after all the bedroom rodeo activity he'll be experiencing." And he laughed a dirty laugh, winking at Veronica.

Veronica gave him *that* look, shaking her head.

Earlier that very afternoon, the *Fasten Seatbelts* sign dinged on the TWA Lockheed Constellation, with a stewardess reminding everyone to do just that as they made their final approach into Orly Airport. Peyton Chase pressed his face close to the window, glancing down, seeing the Eiffel Tower below him as the airplane made a sharp bank, turning southward toward the airport.

Boyhood friend to Billy Bennett, both men had fought side-by-side as pilots in World War Two, each being severely wounded and each receiving the Purple Heart. The two men had been involved in some near-misses regarding a few Nazi sympathizers while in London three years earlier, and then, the following year, met hazards once again back in the States because of a couple murderous, conniving individuals and a highly-valued old oil painting.

Hoping that all *that* was behind him, Peyton Chase was ready for a little relaxation and a *lot* of romance. The talented young actress from the Soviet Union, Anoushka Markarova, with whom he had become smitten during that harrowing escapade in London a few years earlier would be in Paris for a couple weeks. On behalf of the Gorky Moscow Art Theatre, she would be attending a one-week workshop at the famed Théâtre de l'Oeuvre.

Peyton was disappointed that she wasn't coming to the United States, even though she had a fake French passport under the name of Alexis Morgan. But he would take advantage of the situation at hand. His father and, God forbid, his cousin could handle the gun shop in Dover, New Jersey while he was enjoying the many pleasures of Paris. His libido was primed.

After an eighteen-hour flight that included stops in Gander, Newfoundland and Shannon, Ireland, Peyton Chase was ready for a nap before anything else. He paid the cab driver that had deposited him in front of the Hotel Bristol on Rue de Rivoli, picked up his duffle bag, and strode into the lobby.

"Welcome, monsieur Chase," said the desk clerk as he checked in. "Mademoiselle Markarova checked in yesterday. She went out earlier this morning but asked that I give this note to you upon your arrival."

The desk clerk gave a sly wink to Peyton as he handed the note to him.

As Peyton waited for the elevator to take him up to their room, he carefully tore open the envelope and read the note.

*Rest well, handsome. We won't be getting much sleep tonight.*

Peyton Chase laughed loudly, glanced back at the desk clerk giving him a slight salute and smiled broadly.

Welcome to Paris, indeed!

Following round two of their lovemaking later that evening, a *very* satisfied and sweating Peyton Chase sat up in the bed, leaning back on his elbows as he looked down at Anoushka who was between his spread legs.

"Wow! Ya know, kiddo, I'm pretty sure what you just did is illegal back in the States," he said with a wide smile.

Anoushka giggled.

"Who knows? Perhaps it is here, as well," she replied, shrugging her shoulder.

"Nah, just a wild guess, but I'll bet they invented that over here. And you just perfected it!"

He swung his legs around and hopped off the bed. He padded, naked, over to a small table near the window and picked up the nearly empty bottle of champagne out of the ice bucket. He divided what was left in it between two flute glasses and brought them back to the bed as Anoushka sat up.

"Here's to you and me," he said as he handed a glass to his lover, clinking the glasses together, "…and to round number three!"

# 23

It was a beautiful autumn day as Billy walked toward the Thames, hoping that the old man he'd bought all the fireworks from a few years ago would still be there selling his wares. He had enjoyed chatting with him and learning what Bonfire Night was all about. He passed a few of the old familiar posters advertising the pyrotechnics: Jumping Crackers, Pin Wheels, Pom-Pom Cannons, and Roman Candles. All the things Billy remembered that he had purchased back then.

Then, up ahead, he saw the same old wooden pushcart with the same old grizzled dog lying under it. Billy was elated.

But it was the younger man selling the explosives.

"Hey," Billy said almost with a laugh. "You're the new guy."

He remembered that the man's name was New. Joe New. And had teased the young man about it.

"You're the *new* New guy," Billy said laughing like a hyeana. "Where's the old New guy? Who knew there were two News?"

Joe New simply stared at Billy Bennett like he was a crazy person.

"Are ya daft, matey?" Joe New said, still staring, looking Billy up and down. "Get shell-shocked or sumpin' during the war, did ya, Yank? Or is ya drunk as a skunk?"

Billy stopped laughing.

"I'm sorry," Billy said, suddenly serious. "I bought a bunch of stuff from you and your father a few years ago and, for Pete's sake, obviously you don't remember me. Hell, how *could* you? Why *should* you? You probably sell your crap to hundreds of others."

Joe New continued to stare, and then he just shrugged his shoulders.

"So," Billy began, trying to regain what little composure he thought he had, "are you filling in for your dad today. I remember he was a feisty old coot."

"Me old man. That would be Ralphie," responded Joe New nonchalantly. "Fookin' old sot kicked off a year or so ago, he did. Sittin' right at the fookin' breakfast table, he was. Fell face first into his bubble and squeak. Me mom was pissed. Spoilt the whole day, it did."

The old dog that had been sleeping under the cart woke up and realized someone was nearby. He lifted his head and his tail started thumping on the pavement. Billy bent down and stroked the dog's head and ruffled his ears.

"Jamie, there," Joe New said, pointing down to the dog, "is the only one who misses me old man. And now me old Mum brings a fookin' new bloke home every other week, it seems."

This was *far* more information than Billy Bennett needed to hear. He was almost sorry that he had sought out the New's cart.

"Well…I'm sorry, I guess, for whatever is happening with you," Billy felt obligated to say *something*, but wasn't sure exactly what to say.

He selected a large array of the fireworks, knowing that he'd probably be giving some of them away to the various kids he would pass on the street. Joe New filled up two old rumpled paper sacks with the firecrackers. Billy paid for his purchases, bent down to pet the old dog one more time and then he headed back to Devon's place.

He passed three different groups of happy, giggly little boys while on his walk, each time a young lad would run up to him with the familiar "Penny for the Guy?" Billy tossed a few coins at the boys and distributed a few of the Jumping Crackers to the sheer delight of the kids.

Veronica would be at the theater rehearsing until late, so there was no need to hurry back to Devon's place. Billy Bennett enjoyed his slow, ambling walk through the city, stopping for a freshly baked pasty at a street vendor's cart.

He chuckled when he read the old wooden marquee sign in front of St. John's church a few blocks from Devon's house. Aside from listing the time for the services, the sign boasted a topic that surely would have delighted a writer of murder mysteries: *KNOW WHAT HAPPENS WHEN YOU DIE? COME AND FIND OUT.*

Billy laughed out loud. Obviously the "fookin' old sot" Ralphie New now knew.

He continued on his walk and then thought about his good friend, Peyton, and wondered if he was enjoying his time with Anoushka in Paris.

Peyton Chase was enjoying *every* minute with Anoushka and didn't give a single solitary thought about his good friend Billy Bennett.

# 24

*November 5, 1955*
*Bonfire Night*

With opening night just a few nights away, Veronica Barron was still at the theater rehearsing and would be for several more hours. Billy Bennett was out in front of Devon's house acting like a ten-year-old setting off the firecrackers that he had bought earlier in the day. A small group of neighborhood kids joined him and they all bounced around like floppy marionettes on strings when the explosives shot off.

*Can't wait to have kids of my own* Billy Bennett thought.

After fits and starts, Devon Stone sat at his desk; once again typing the beginning of chapter ten in his new murder mystery. It had taken him months to get even this far. He had written, rewritten, stopped, started, thrown away and restarted again several times. His creative juices had stalled, and it distressed him. His previous books, all of them best sellers, had come easily and he had played his typewriter like a Stradivarius. Not so now. He wasn't even totally satisfied yet with his working title of *Dressed to Kill*. Having enjoyed the company of a very dapper detective in New York City when he was last there, he is turning the very real, the very congenial Lieutenant James Lafferty into a fictitious central character who gets introduced in this chapter. He chuckled to himself while he wrote, as a small cloud of smoke with the distinct aroma of cannabis swirled around his head.

It hadn't gotten dark yet, but already he heard the sounds of firecrackers being set off up and down his normally quiet street. He shook his head knowing that that crazy Yank, Billy Bennett, was out there enjoying this holiday just like his own Fourth of July shenanigans back in the States. Londoners take Bonfire Night very seriously. He glanced at his watch as he heard his front doorbell ring. Being that his friend was out front, he hadn't locked the door.

"Blast," he muttered. "Broke my train of thought. Not that I was even on the right track, at that. Can't Billy get back in?"

It was slightly past cocktail hour and he figured he'd fix himself a nice gin and tonic after answering the door.

A handsome, well-dressed young man, looking to be around his mid twenties, smiled as Devon opened the door. Devon glanced down at the street and Billy was still out there, surrounded by a throng of gleeful youngsters waiting for more firecrackers to be set off.

"Good evening, Mr. Stone," he said, tipping his hat, as he handed a small package to the author.

Devon stepped back for a moment. A flashback to another package, albeit left on his doorstep, two years earlier. He glanced at it. No ticking sounds. No *Memento Mori* scribbled across the surface of the wrapping.

"This is from solicitor Blackstone's office, sir. I was asked to deliver this to you and requested that you sign for its receipt."

The young man handed the package to Devon, along with a clipboard and a pen.

Devon hesitated for a brief moment, and then signed the attached form.

"It's an honor to meet you, Mr. Stone," said the young man with a huge smile. "I'm Jesse Thorndike and I've read all of your books, sir. Actually, even more than once or twice."

"I'm flattered, Jesse Thorndike," Devon responded with an even larger smile. "I have no idea who this Mr. Blackstone is, but I'm sure I'm about to find out."

"Yes, sir," Jesse Thorndike said, tipping his hat once again and nodding as he turned to go back down the steps. "Sounds like a war zone out here already, doesn't it? Enjoy the holiday, Mr. Stone."

After closing his front door, Devon shook the package. No sound. Nothing rattling. No ticking bomb seemed to be waiting within.

Devon Stone poured himself a healthy-sized gin and tonic at his bar and carried the package under his arm as he climbed the stairs back to his office. Standing at his desk, he laid the package down, stared at it for a moment, and sipped his drink. The package, firmly wrapped in brown paper and tied with twine, intrigued him. He took another sip and began to unwrap it. There was a cardboard box under the wrappings and he slowly, cautiously lifted the lid. Inside the box was a lengthy handwritten note sitting on top of what looked like a manuscript. Before he read the note, he glanced at the top page...the title page...of the manuscript.

*YOU CAN'T GO IN THERE!* A Thriller by Samuel Fleck.

Devon Stone knew this man. A friend. A fellow author. And the one who had committed suicide six months earlier.

Loud fireworks started exploding outside as Devon Stone suddenly plopped down into his chair. He started reading the note.

"Bloody hell!" he exclaimed as he read.

*My dear friend, Devon,*

*I am dead. And soon you will be as well if you are not cautious, being that you now hold my final manuscript in your hands. My fears may have been realized. In the event of my untimely demise, I have instructed my solicitor to deliver this package to you six months from the date of my death. Being that you are now reading this, you may assume that I now know what lies on the other side. If anything. Obviously I was foolish to not follow up on my suspicions. If my death has been ruled a suicide, that is incorrect. I have grown to distrust my own son. He has been distant, both in emotion and miles, for years. Certain circumstances lead me to believe he has grown to despise me and may be plotting something sinister. Please read the enclosed manuscript. By receiving this package, it will mean that I have not yet sent it to our respective publisher, James Flynn. Be aware, Devon, that the pages are explosive in their exposé, albeit somewhat fictitiously.*

*Please, dear friend, solve my murder.*

*See you again sometime on the other side, maybe.*

*Warmest regards,*
*Sam*

Devon Stone finished reading the note and, sitting back in his chair, he simply shook his head.

"Hmmm...interesting," he said out loud to no one but himself. "Certainly bizarre to say the least."

A few more fireworks exploded somewhere in the distance.

He leaned forward, laid the note on his desk and stared at it. And thought about it.

*This just doesn't seem to make sense,* Devon thought to himself.

He remembered the so-called suicide note that Jeremy Fleck had shown him the night of that strange memorial service. He remembered the handwriting. The note that he had just finished reading was obviously written by a left-handed person. The "suicide note" was not.

*Or, is my imagination working overtime? Let's just see what this might reveal,* he thought as he picked up the manuscript and started to read *YOU CAN'T GO IN THERE* by Samuel Fleck.

By the time Devon was halfway through the manuscript he was getting concerned.

He was finding the piece neither explosive nor licentious in nature. If, indeed, it was intended as a roman à clef as James Flynn, their respective publisher had told him, Devon Stone couldn't figure out who the characters might be in reality.

Save for two.

Aside from that, he was finding the writing to be horrible. Extremely pedestrian and unexciting. In fact, it crossed the border from boring to sleep inducing with ease. Just like the last three of Samuel Fleck's books.

The plot, flimsy and trite as it was, involved the plotting and execution of a major art museum heist involving a wealthy old man (the mastermind thief), a rag-tag group of his accomplices, and his prissy, wayward, unloving son.

In alternating chapters, each relayed in the first-person, the story vacillated back and forth in point of view between the father and son, with each one eventually thinking that the other was trying to thwart his actions.

The further Devon read, the more it became apparent, no matter how poorly written it was, that the son was plotting to murder his father.

Two hours later Devon Stone was still reading the manuscript when Billy Bennett came up the stairs and walked into the office.

"Well," Billy said with a huge grin, "those little neighborhood kiddies sure enjoyed all that noise. So did I. I love this holiday of yours!"

"You smell of gun powder, Billy. Or, rather the residue of those blasted firecrackers. No pun intended", snickered Devon. "Are you finished for the night now or are you about to go back outside and set off a bonfire someplace trying to burn London down?"

"Nah, I'm done. I'll just wait until Ronnie gets back from the theater. Did I interrupt your reading? Or writing? Or whatever else you might have been doing?"

Devon Stone sat back in his chair once again, taking a long sip of his third drink. He lifted the manuscript in the air for Billy to see.

"This is the final manuscript from my departed friend, Samuel Fleck. And this may just help prove something I've thought about, off and on, for the past six months," he said shaking his head. "Something I was afraid of."

"And that would be?" Billy asked.

"My friend's death really may *not* have been suicide after all."

"Oh? Then what was it?" asked Billy, cocking his head.

"It may have been patricide," answered Devon with a frown.

"What's that?" asked Billy.

"Another word for murder," Devon said.

# 25

The following morning, after calling for an abrupt appointment, Devon Stone was sitting in James Flynn's office. He wanted to share this strange manuscript and note with someone who also might have had doubts about Fleck's suicide.

"I'm convinced, James", said Devon, as he handed the handwritten piece of stationery to his publisher, "more than ever, that Jeremy Fleck killed his father. Take a look at this note Sam sent to me from beyond the grave."

James Flynn read the note as his eyebrows arched higher and higher.

"This certainly *seems* to raise that issue, Devon, doesn't it? But it's not definitive enough to really place the blame on anyone. Not yet, anyway. Not that I can see."

"But it's not *what* was written, James, but *how* it was written."

James Flynn cocked his head and frowned.

"Meaning what, exactly, Devon?"

"Look at the handwriting, James. This was obviously written by a left-handed person. Any handwriting expert will attest to that. The *supposed* suicide note, or apology note or whatever he called it that Jeremy Fleck showed to me was *not* written the same way."

James Flynn sat back, sighed, and pursed his lips. He paused a moment before speaking.

"Well," said Flynn clearing his throat. "Well, well, well. I may have to redirect your way of thinking regarding *that* issue, Stone. Samuel Fleck was ambidextrous. He could write, equally as well, both left and right handed. I saw it in person on several occasions. And, so of course the handwriting would definitely look different."

"What the hell," exclaimed Devon. "I never knew that!"

James Flynn laughed out loud.

"You mean to tell me, that the great Devon Stone who knows things because he's a writer *didn't* know that little tidbit of trivia?"

"Oh, fuck it, Flynn. There goes *one* theory out the window."

Silence for a moment. The two men sat and stared at each other.

"But I *still* have my doubts about it being a suicide," said Devon.

James Flynn simply shrugged his shoulders.

Jian Hyui sat and stared out of the filthy window in his bedroom. The sun was going down and he debated whether or not to head across the street to Kowloon Walled City. The rehearsal for the latest opera had gone well. The music still swirled around in his head and he hummed a few bars as he sat there.

He made a decision. He stood up.

He sharpened his two long blades and then changed his clothes.

Tormenting thoughts churned around in his head. Thoughts of Jeremy Fleck and what he had said. Thoughts of Samuel Fleck and what he had *done*.

Jeremy Fleck had seemed to be aware of what Jian had done or *was* doing.

*Have I been followed?* Jian Hyui thought to himself. *Will I be followed tonight?*

But tonight he would try to be vigilant.

He just wasn't vigilant enough.

# 26

Despite the fact that there were still a few lingering doubts, apparently the authorities were sticking with their original ruling of suicide. For now, anyway.

But Devon Stone had questions. So many questions...too many questions. It wasn't any of his business, he realized, but he simply couldn't get his *own* lingering thoughts of murder versus suicide out of his head. He felt as though he needed to confront Jeremy Fleck but thought that it would be awkward doing so in the man's own residence. Although, actually, it was still his deceased father's residence. But nonetheless, Devon figured it would be in poor taste. He called Samuel Fleck's old telephone number and was pleasantly surprised when it was answered. It was answered by a female voice.

"Good afternoon," said Devon, "This is Devon Stone, and would I be speaking to Beth Barnes, by any chance?"

There was a slight pause on the other end of the line before Samuel Fleck's housekeeper answered.

"Why, yes, Mr. Stone," she answered. "I can't believe you remembered my name. We met for only the briefest of moments and that was several months ago."

Although he could have, Devon Stone would never tell her that he could recall, verbatim, conversations he had when he was five years old. She probably wouldn't believe him anyway.

"I hope I'm not intruding on anything," responded Devon, "but I was trying to reach Jeremy Fleck. Has he returned to Hong Kong yet or is he still available?"

"Jer...ah, Mr. Fleck is trying to clear up some things still here in London. He just returned from Hong Kong yesterday. I'm tidying up the place before I move on to other employment. I assume you would much prefer speaking with Mr. Fleck than me, Mr. Stone. Please hold on and I'll see if I can locate him. I heard him rumbling around somewhere upstairs a few moments ago."

Devon heard the sound as she laid the telephone receiver on a table. He was also certain he heard music playing in the background. The music stopped suddenly. And footsteps were heard, as they seemed to be approaching the telephone.

"This is Jeremy Fleck," came the terse response.

"Good afternoon, Jeremy. I don't know if Miss Barnes told you it was me or not..."

"She did so, Devon. I assume that you've been well since we last spoke. What's on your mind?"

*Well, then, why not just cut to the chase,* thought Devon Stone.

"I'd like to invite you to drop by my house for a drink or two. I'm still stunned by your loss and I think we should get to know each other a bit better. Your father kept you quite a secret."

"My father kept a *lot* of secrets, Devon. A lot."

Awkward silence.

"Yes, well..." Devon continued. "Be that as it may. By any chance, would you be available this evening around six-ish for drinks and a chat? I could prepare a light meal as well. I really *would* like to get to know you better."

Jeremy Fleck was not an idiot. He was extremely intuitive and his instincts kicked in. He knew there had to be an ulterior motive for a meeting. But he was not concerned.

"Actually, Devon, as luck would have it I've lost track of the time today and hadn't planned anything for dinner. I'd enjoy a drink or two with you.

Please don't go to the trouble of preparing a meal or anything. Perhaps we could both go out for a bite afterwards."

"Jolly good," said Devon Stone.

He gave Jeremy Fleck his address, although he knew Fleck already had it, and ended the call.

"I realize that Veronica will be at the theater until quite late again this evening," Devon said as he paced in front of Billy Bennett. "Please don't take this as me being rude in any way…although, I guess, it is. I'm expecting a guest this evening and…"

"Ah, hah!" exclaimed Billy, with a silly smirk and a sly wink. "Let me guess. It's your lady friend that I have yet to meet and you want me to be…"

"No, no, no, not that at all," interrupted Devon. "This could potentially be a very dicey situation. The son of my deceased friend will be stopping by around six. Words could be used that might require raised voices. Tensions could rise. I may make some strong accusations. Then again, maybe not depending upon how things go. I certainly don't expect him to stay very long, again, depending upon the conversation. So if you would please just…"

"I know, I know" chuckled Billy. "Just stay in my room like a good little boy. I'll take one of your books in there with me and maybe some crayons. I should be asleep and snoring in no time."

Devon gave him a withering look.

"But if you should hear any gunshots, Billy, you *might* want to alert the authorities."

The evening would *not* turn out the way Devon was anticipating. Not. At. All.

At five-forty five Devon Stone paced in his living room, wondering if he might offer Fleck a special "smoke" or two along with a drink or two. Might loosen him up a bit and make him more willing to talk. Or to confess. Then Devon wondered if he should carry a small, concealed pistol…just in case Fleck would attack out of anger and desperation. After all, Samuel had warned Devon in the note that danger might be at hand if he was not cautious.

*Then* he wondered why he should have even bothered to get this involved. He's expected to *write* mysteries, not *solve* them. But the die had been cast.

*We'll just have to see how things play out,* he thought to himself.

At six-fifteen, Devon Stone greeted Jeremy Fleck at his front door.

The two men exchanged the usual pleasantries as Devon ushered Fleck into his large parlor off of the main hallway.

"Magnificent artwork, Mr. Stone," remarked Jeremy Fleck as he perused the paintings that were hung on every wall. From an early Picasso to a late Kandinsky, a rather tantalizing Gustav Klimt from his "Golden Phase", and with a very red Rothko thrown into the middle somewhere just for the fun of it. They were just some of Devon's prized possessions.

"I'm impressed," Jeremy continued as he strolled around glancing at each painting. "I much prefer *this* kind of collection as opposed to the old stodgy crap my parents hung around their place. Obviously you're a collector of the very best."

"Oh, I dabble a bit," chuckled Devon, as he headed toward his bar. "What's your…", he had started to ask *what's your poison?*, then instantly decided that was a poor choice of words, considering the circumstances. "…drink of choice, Jeremy?"

"Do you know how to make a Vesper Martini, by any chance?"

Devon Stone laughed.

"Bloody hell," he said, still laughing. "Are you serious? A former associate of mine in MI6, and a fellow author, was the one who created that drink. He loved it so much he mentioned it in his first novel, *Casino Royale,* a couple years ago. Perhaps you may have read it?"

"I didn't know you were in MI6, Devon. Now I'm *really* impressed."

"I was associated with it to some degree during the war. I keep *that* part of my life sort of secret. No need to go into any details. Yes, to answer your question, I certainly know how to make your cocktail. I, myself, prefer gin and tonics but I think I will join you with one of those drinks. Potent, to say the least. We just may be roaring drunk before we know it!"

And they both laughed.

*And just maybe I* will *get a drunken confession out of you yet,* Devon thought.

Devon Stone could hold his alcohol very well. He didn't know about Jeremy Fleck.

Devon prepared the drinks, poured them and they toasted to each other's health.

Devon cleared his throat after the first sip. He wanted to bait his guest carefully.

"Jeremy, I still feel very remorseful regarding your late father. I regret not being a better friend to him. I didn't really know what kind of life he had aside from his writings." *Although the writing was plainly on the wall,* Devon thought.

Jeremy Fleck downed his drink almost in one gulp. Devon hesitated a moment and then followed suit.

"I won't even ask if you'd care for another," said Devon, "I should probably make a pitcher of these things."

He made another cocktail for each of them.

Jeremy sat back in a large, comfortable albeit very modern chair, sipping his drink more slowly this time.

"My father," said Jeremy Fleck, "had far more secrets than you could ever imagine. He thought he had kept them well hidden from both my late mother and me. He didn't. He had far more *faults* than you could ever imagine. He did damaging things to those who loved him the most. I was one of them. If you knew my father, as you claim, you must have been aware that he was an unfaithful husband. In several ways. And with both genders."

Another awkward silence.

"I suspected as such, Jeremy, I'm embarrassed to say. Certain observations were made, and then set aside. I have recently been made aware of such an incident."

Jeremy Fleck sighed and nodded his head. He knew *exactly* the incident to which Devon referred, but he would let that situation remain untouched for the moment.

Devon wanted to pick up the pace of this conversation, not knowing where it might lead. Yet, he wanted to play it cautiously. He had been hoping for frankness, which appeared to be happening, but he realized an actual confession to murder would probably not be forthcoming. But if it did, then *his* life would be…or could be in jeopardy.

"Another drink, Jeremy?"

"Of course. You make them only too well, Devon. Do you have a private source for Kina Lillet? It's hard to find."

"My off-licence keeps me very well supplied," answered Devon as he prepared a third drink for each of them. "I entertain a lot and I suppose I practically keep them in business."

He handed the fresh drink to Jeremy and took a sip from his own.

*Time to get down to* this *business,* he thought.

"All right, Jeremy," Devon said, collecting his thoughts, as he paced back and forth in front of the young man. "You might be thinking that this is absolutely none of my damn business and you might be *absolutely* correct. I certainly don't know what issues you may have had with your father, but *I'd* like to resolve one issue right now. And, please, spare me the melodrama. I want the truth. No matter how it hurts."

Jeremy Fleck stood up and faced Devon Stone squarely in his eyes. Apparently they were each beginning to feel the effects of the potent drink. The air became instantly intense. It had the potential for a cockfight.

Jeremy reached into his pocket and Devon reacted, wondering if a pistol or knife was about to be drawn. But the man simply pulled out a handkerchief to wipe his lips.

"Then *you'd* better have a seat, Mr. Stone. This may take a while and I wouldn't want you to pass out from the shock."

"I write some pretty gruesome murder mysteries, Fleck. Nothing shocks me."

Jeremy chuckled.

"We'll see, won't we?"

Devon Stone sat as Jeremy started to pace.

"First of all, Devon, I must clear up the use of that word 'issue'. You inferred that I had…hmmm…father issues. Many sons do, I understand. Lasting for years. In my case, however, it was the other way around. He had issues with *me*. I shall explain those further on, but I shall address first things first."

Devon Stone stared, unblinking, at Jeremy Fleck.

"You're very intuitive and I'm sure you may have figured out by now, Devon, that I lied at that memorial service for my father."

"Ah, ha! I suspected as much. So then, you did *not* write those last three dreadful books."

"That, sir, is absolutely correct. I did not. But…"

He paused.

Devon waited.

"I *did* write the first three successful ones."

# 27

Devon Stone sat, mouth agape. Both he and Jeremy Fleck held a stare. Devon downed his drink. That was *not* what Devon had been expecting to hear.

"Wait. What? All right. Let's set the record straight. Samuel Fleck published six books," Devon finally said. "How many of those did *he* actually write?"

"I just told you, Devon. Three. The final three."

"And what about those *first* three?"

Jeremy Fleck decided to pull up a chair and bring it in close to Devon's side.

"It started as a lark, Devon. A harmless joke. Early on in life Father had been a fairly competent accountant, earning a decent wage. He had always had the desire to write but, God bless him, he hadn't the talent."

"But…" Devon almost uncharacteristically stammered. "Those first three became best-sellers. Each one selling more than the previous. I don't…I simply don't get what's going on here. I don't get what you're trying to tell me."

"I'm not *trying* to tell you, Devon, I *am* telling you. Please listen…then comment or bash me in my bloody face."

They sat back into their respective chairs and sighed.

"It was just something silly that got out of hand, Devon. It really was *extremely* stupid on our parts, when you think about it. And could have been disastrous right from the start. Father had written several manuscripts prior to this…all of which were roundly and soundly rejected by one publisher after another. Justifiably so. He gave me some minor thoughts about a plot and, in my spare time, I wrote a murder mystery called *Open Verdict*. He thought it was brilliant and urged me to send it off to some publishing house to see what might happen. I scoffed at it and foolishly… kiddingly, *drunkenly* told him to send it off himself with his name as the author. It was a preposterous suggestion, of course. We had a bloody good laugh and several more stiff drinks over that one. Never, ever thinking that he would actually do it. And, so…he did it. Lo and behold, he sent it off to Dartmouth Press. The one publishing house he *hadn't* sent all his other shit to. And James Flynn loved it. The rest, as they say, is cliché, cliché, etc."

The air became deathly still. As if neither man was breathing.

"And then?" asked Devon Stone.

"And then," answered Jeremy Fleck, "ah, yes…and then. Neither one of us wanted to tell this publisher, poor unsuspecting Mr. Flynn, the truth. We were scared to. We thought the deal would be cancelled outright if we told the truth. Or worse. There were lawyers and contracts involved at this point. In essence, we were committing fraud of some sort. False representation. We thought we could be sued into bankruptcy perhaps. So we said 'what the hell, eh?' Let's see how this thing plays out. It was just going to be a one-time thing. To say that we were thunderstruck is an understatement to beat all."

"But…" started Devon, still in disbelief, "what were *your* true emotions going through at that time?"

"Listen, I sincerely loved and respected my old Dad. When I was a wee tyke he was a very loving man and a very decent father. We had a lot of fun together. Many good times. As I matured through the years, though, I slowly became aware of his…umm…proclivities. But he was my father and I still loved him. I let him have his blaze of glory. Well, what I thought would be his *one* blaze of glory, that is, and that would be it. It would be over. I sat back and simply enjoyed the glow from it. Many people often seek credit for success, justified or not. I did not. And very few will accept responsibility for failure. Father did…in the bitter end unfortunately."

"But," Devon repeated, "Obviously, then, you must have written two *more* books following *that* remarkable success. And still remaining quiet about it? You certainly deserve the prize for the world's most noble son or the world's greatest liar. Or both. Every single writer I know has an ego the size of an elephant. Some, a pack of elephants."

"Honestly, when the manuscript for the second book was presented we *could* have claimed joint authorship at that point and gotten away with it, but the subject never arose. I neither needed nor wanted the notoriety at that time, Devon. Seriously. I was, and still am, simply content and successful doing what I did on a daily basis since the end of the war."

"Which is?"

"I'm a journalist, Devon. I'm surprised you hadn't asked this long before now. I'm an editor and correspondent in the Hong Kong office for The Times. Ironic, isn't it? I cover both the financial and the crime scenes. Sometimes they overlap."

"This is getting far more convoluted than *any* of my novels," exclaimed Devon, throwing up his arms.

Jeremy Fleck stood up once again and started pacing.

"Wait. You ain't heard nothin' yet, Devon, as the late, great Al Jolson once said. By that time, my father's life had changed. He was a success, albeit falsely. No one but he and I knew that."

Devon's mind was spinning. Was he being fed the largest possible plateful of bullshit? Or was this seemingly unbelievable tale factual? Jeremy Fleck had far more to reveal. Would it end up in a confession for his father's murder or did Samuel Fleck really and truly die by his own hand?

Devon Stone made another drink for each of them.

Jian Hyui had previously and carelessly waited until his potential attackers had crept up closely behind him before he lashed out. Tonight he was feeling emboldened. *I was born in the year of the snake* he thought. *I neither forgive, nor forget.* He slowly walked through the narrow, filthy passageways of Kowloon Walled City, dressed as usual in the garb of an old woman. But tonight he wasn't planning on being the unsuspecting prey. No, tonight he was the prowler. The stalker. He had more dragons to slay.

But he wasn't aware, however, that this time he *was* being followed.

"As soon as *Open Verdict* hit the best-seller lists, Devon, a switch was flicked somewhere in my father's pitiful demented mind. The success surprised him. Hell, it surprised the *both* of us. Instantly he was beginning to get quite a following and his ego, although erroneously, was inflated. He became frightened that I would betray him. That I would divulge the truth. He would be exposed as a hack writer. Or worse. I assured him that I would never do that. His secret...*our* secret was secure forever. Besides, the legality of the whole thing was still an issue. We both were committing fraud. He became more and more distant, even as I continued to write the next books for him."

Devon Stone's mind raced.

"Before you continue, Fleck...and I implore you, please *do* continue. I see a weird irony in this whole situation."

"That being?" asked Jeremy Fleck.

"Your father's death has been ostensibly ruled a suicide. At this point, for no other reason than a gut feeling, I doubt that calling. The irony? The title of your father's first book...*your* first book. *Open Verdict*. You wrote about it, so obviously you know what it means."

The dictionary definition of "open verdict" is an option open to a coroner's jury at an inquest in the legal system of England and Wales. The verdict means that the jury confirms that the death is suspicious; a crime *may* have been committed, while not naming a criminal, and not specifying the actual cause of death.

"Obviously, of course," answered Fleck. "I based all three of those books *very* loosely on a few of the cases I had been following in the press over the years and taking great artistic license. The case upon which I based *Open Verdict* turned out, in reality, to be a true suicide although I had turned it into a murder in the book."

"I remember the book well, Fleck," said Devon Stone, still perplexed.

"The devious plot involved innocuous medication being switched with poison in pill form. Actually, very similar to the very first Sherlock Holmes book, *A Study in Scarlet*. Intriguing coincidence. That's why you *could* have been in Hong Kong, as you insist that you were, and still committed a murder."

Jeremy Fleck stood back, standing erect, folded his arms and glowered at Devon Stone.

Devon Stone realized he was too far away from that desk drawer and his pistol if Fleck decided to do anything rash. He *could* resort to the martial arts, in which he was quite proficient, if necessary. But then that might damage some of his expensive furniture.

"Now I'll ask *you*, Mr. Stone," Jeremy Fleck said with an edge of anger in his tone, "Why are you *so* convinced that my father's death was murder? And, Mr. Mystery Writer, what motive could *I* possibly have had for killing my father? Yes, I lied at the memorial service, but that was to protect my father's legacy with his faithful readers. I didn't lie to protect my own."

"Things are beginning to get a bit tense here, Fleck," Devon said, trying to ratchet down the emotions a bit. "It's my fault, granted, but I fail to see how you do *not* think that something is rotten in the state of Denmark, as the expression goes."

"I shall swear on a stack of bibles in court, sir, I did not…emphatically, did *not* murder my father."

*Someone sure as hell did*, thought Devon Stone. *And my bet is still on you, Jeremy Fleck.*

Jian Hyui saw a small person walking towards him in the darkened alleyway. Obviously a woman, and probably not a fearful, treacherous gang member. He kept his head down, to avoid being detected as a man in woman's clothing, and stepped aside to politely let the woman pass by. She was wearing a long hooded robe of some sort, which Hyui thought odd but *anything goes in this place* he thought.

The woman approached, slowed down, and then stopped directly in front of him.

"Tíng xià! *Stop!* What do you think you are doing?" she asked, her face still hooded in darkness.

He recognized that voice. And he stepped back, stunned.

# 28

"Sifu Lau!" Jian Hyui exclaimed in horror. "Master, why are you here?"

Lau lowered her hood uncovering her face and glowered at Hyui.

"I have had my suspicions about the murders here in this wretched place," Lau answered sorrowfully. "The violent ones seem to have begun soon after I entrusted you with the knives...which I know you have concealed beneath your garments even now. I have been following you."

Jian Hyui didn't know what to make of this touchy situation. He was just accused of committing horrendous murders by the one who taught him how to do it.

He started to speak but was interrupted and startled by the sound of a young male voice coming up behind him.

"Will you take a look at this, guys," said the voice. "Two little old ladies stopping for a chat."

Lau peered around Jian's shoulders and saw three nasty-looking young men sauntering towards them.

"I'll just bet you girls would like to make a sizeable donation to our cause, wouldn't you?" All three punks laughed like hyenas. Then they extended their right arms, fists clenched, toward one another. The Triad hand signal for *together*.

"And your cause would be?" asked Lau coyly. She was getting prepared.

"Ha!" laughed the first punk. "*Be*-cause. Because I said so, right, guys?"

He slowly pulled a meat cleaver from his jacket. Jian Hyui had still not turned around to face the trio. As far as they knew, he was just another helpless old lady.

"Is that pitiful little weapon meant to frighten us?" Lau asked sarcastically as she stepped closer to the man with the cleaver. "Or are you here to behead some chickens for your dinners?"

Lau was showing great sangfroid, which seemed to embolden Jian Hyui.

"Oh, a spunky little old bitch, aren't you?" snarled the man as he stepped even closer to Lau, taking a menacing position.

Lau could smell the foul breath of her adversary and she winked at Jian.

"I think it might be time to let that cat out of that sack once again," Jian Hyui whispered to Lau.

"What did you just say, you filthy old crone?" one of the other punks said from behind the first guy as he punched Jian's shoulder.

"I said," Jian Hyui yelled loudly as he spun around so quickly that the trio of gang members hardly saw the motion, "Prepare to meet Shàngdì, you bastards!"

Both he and Lau retrieved their long knives from beneath their respective garments and took their battle stance.

The three young men, dressed in tight black trousers and shirts, stepped back in shock. This was certainly an unexpected change of circumstances. The situation had suddenly been altered. Two of them pulled shorts knives from their trouser pockets and prepared to do battle. The man with the meat cleaver rushed, foolishly, toward Lau.

Lau swung one blade and knocked the cleaver from the attackers hand, severing two of his fingers as she did so. He screamed, more from shock and surprise than from pain. He scrambled to pick up his cleaver again. Unfortunately his neck got in the way of one of Jian's blades as he swung it swiftly slicing the man's jugular vein on the left side. Before he had even hit the ground, his other two companions rushed toward Lau.

Taking a stance, she swung her two long knives as if in a well-choreographed dance, striking a hard blow to one of her attackers on the side of his head slicing off the top of his ear while doing so. A long gash opened up and blood flowed swiftly down his neck. Her other knife sliced straight across the top of his head effectively scalping him. His long black monk's braid went flying into the gutter.

The third man took too much time watching his fellow punks fall to the ground in bloody heaps. He almost never felt Jian Hyui's blade as it was thrust into his chest, piercing his sternum and dividing his heart into two pieces.

Lau and Hyui stared at each other.

"Kuài diǎn! Kuài pǎo!" *Hurry! Run fast!* Lau shouted. And they both ran from Kowloon Walled City.

Ten minutes later, still out of breath from both the combat and the running, Lau and Jian Hyui stood side by side at the railing of a Star Ferry. It was almost halfway across Victoria Harbour. Lightning flickered in the sky overhead.

Jian tearfully explained why he was doing what he had done. He explained about his young, beautiful friend Meili.

"I am so sorry, Sifu Lau, I have betrayed your masterful and honorable teachings. I have become a murderer. Like the Triads that lurk in the shadows."

"Quiet, Hyui," said Lau, shaking her head. "I reasoned that you must have had a solid purpose behind your doings. I have watched how you changed. It distressed me. But…" She paused to take a breath. "You did what I could not."

"I do not understand, sifu Lau," Jian said with a confused look on his face. "What do you mean by that?"

Lau was silent, downcast, and wondered if she should even say what was on her mind. She sighed heavily and looked toward the sky before speaking.

"One of the Triads, I know not which…makes no difference. They are all the same wretched human beings. One of the Triads," she continued, "robbed and beat my poor elderly father mercilessly a couple years ago. I loved that man so deeply. He never recovered, dying from severe internal injuries a week later. I wanted revenge. *Oh*, how I wanted revenge! My mother forbade me from going into that place. She told me revenge was wrong. Revenge was for the weak of spirit and mind. I honored my mother's request. She died from old age earlier this year. What I suspected you of doing renewed my anger and hatred toward the gangs that roam in there."

Jian Hyui stared at this seemingly fragile, now openly weeping woman in disbelief.

"What we just did was wrong, Hyui. So *very* wrong. We let our emotions take over our senses of wrong and right. Wrong won out. We have both just committed murder," Lau said wistfully. "And now it *must* stop. Do you hear me? Our loved ones have been avenged enough. We must never, ever speak of this to anyone. Maybe we will feel guilty for the rest of our lives. Then again, maybe not. I am proud, Hyui, that I taught you well. Now put your anger behind you, as I must."

She looked around to make sure that the few passengers on the ferry were a safe distance away and not paying any attention to the two of them. She motioned for Jian to follow her. They stepped to the rear of the gently rolling boat.

"Together," she said, as she carefully removed the bloody knives from beneath her hooded robe.

Lightning flickered overhead, but the rumble of thunder was distant. The storm had moved past.

Jian Hyui knew what Lau intended and he, too, removed the knives from his long, flowing garments. They turned their backs to the passengers up front.

And simultaneously dropped their knives into the middle of Victoria Harbour.

Devon Stone was feeling a bit more drunk than he had in a long time. And a bit more brazen as well. He could tell by Jeremy Fleck's eyes that the feeling was mutual.

"Okay, Fleck," he said with just a hint of a slur. "Now I'll get to the reason why I asked you here this evening. Apparently your father had his solicitor send his final manuscript to me. He specified that it had to be six months following his death, for some reason. At this point, I haven't a clue why. It certainly was very odd and confusing to me. I took it as a warning of sorts. Perhaps I'm being way too cavalier regarding my own safety at this very moment by bringing this up. But I honestly think he feared that you were going to do him harm and he used this for proof. Or at least something for the authorities to pursue."

Jeremy Fleck just stared at Devon Stone in astonishment.

"What in the holy fuck are you talking about, Stone?"

Devon produced the manuscript in question from a cabinet drawer, and handed it to Jeremy Fleck. He went back to standing by the cabinet. His pistol was in the top drawer.

"Take a look, lad," he said to Jeremy, "But be forewarned. I have a pistol within my grasp should you try anything foolish."

Jeremy Fleck was incredulous.

Jeremy Fleck took the manuscript from Devon Stone's hand. He began flipping through the pages as a confused look crossed his face.

"What in bloody hell are you doing here, Stone?" he asked. "Is this a fucking joke?"

Devon Stone was now the one with a confused look on his face.

"I don't understand, Fleck? What's the problem here?"

"The problem here is that this is *not* my father's supposedly last book. The book you *claim* proves that I murdered him. Or plotted to, anyway."

"What the hell is it, then?" asked Devon.

"It's one of those wretched very first manuscripts that Father wrote. One of the ones rejected by a dozen publishers."

Devon drew his head back in surprise.

"What the bloody hell?" said an equally incredulous Devon Stone.

"Exactly!" exclaimed Jeremy Fleck. "What the bloody hell? It's typed up on Father's old, long since discarded typewriter. I can tell because I recognize all the misshapen S's and the filled in O's."

"But what about this note that came along with it?" asked Devon as he handed the handwritten note of warning from Samuel Fleck. "Now I'm *really* confused."

Jeremy Fleck took the note and read it, shaking his head. He tossed the note into the air and watched as it fluttered to the floor.

"This isn't even my father's handwriting. I repeat, what the hell, Stone?"

"But...well, I was confused when I saw it and remembered the suicide note that you showed me at his memorial service. Two different handwritings, I know, but I was told that your father was ambidextrous. He *was* ambidextrous, wasn't he?"

Jeremy Fleck stood back and stared at Devon Stone.

"I repeat again. Is this a *fucking* joke? My father could barely write legibly with *one* hand, let alone with his other. If he *was* ambidextrous, he kept *that* secret from me along with all his *other* quote-unquote secrets!"

Perplexed, Devon Stone shook his head and it was like a snow globe; all the things he had just heard swirling around in his mind like little tiny flakes in a blur, trying to float down and settle into a composed scenario that made sense. He started pacing back and forth. A thought came to him.

"Supposedly, Jeremy, your father was home alone, just sitting peacefully reading one of my earlier books when he initiated the Grim Reaper to come calling. Do you happen to remember what that book was?"

Furrowing his brows, Fleck took a moment to think about what Beth Barnes, his father's housekeeper, had told the police and told him.

"Yes, it was *Wheels Within Wheels*. A twisty, puzzling one that I recall fondly. An espionage thriller involving spies, and the German Enigma machine from World War Two. And, for what it's worth, it's my favorite of yours."

"Ah, yes, that one was written with the help of a lot of intelligence information gathered from a couple good friends of mine," Devon answered. "But that's beside the point. It's not the content; it's the actual *copy* of that book itself that has me intrigued. That, and your father's handwriting."

"Evidently," continued Jeremy Fleck, "you had inscribed the book."

Devon Stone stopped pacing. His forehead creased in concentration. A long, silent pause. Thoughts were still tumbling through his mind, indeed, like wheels within wheels. He slowly started pacing once more and then suddenly stopped. The snowflakes had settled. The scenario made sense. The hairs on the back of his neck bristled. His eyes shot back to Jeremy Fleck and he looked the man in the eye. He slapped the palms of his hands together.

"Jeremy Fleck, it was *not* suicide, just as I had suspected. If I can verify what I'm thinking at this moment I may have just solved your father's murder. But neither one of us is going to like it one little bit."

# 29

And *now*, at last, the guilt and remorse came.

Guilt can be crippling. Or…it can be liberating.

After crossing back again over Victoria Harbour and slowly, morosely walking the streets leading to his building, Jian Hyui sluggishly trudged up the rickety stairway to his apartment. He reached the fourth floor landing and stopped for a moment, glancing toward the apartment door where young, beautiful Meili had once lived. He heard the distant rumble of thunder as the brief storm swept past. Thunderstorms were rare this late in the season, but he gave it no thought.

He quietly opened his own door, turned on the light in his entranceway and nearly collapsed from anguish. His mind began racing. He sat down on the small hassock, buried his face in his hands and wept loudly.

*What have I done?* Hyui thought.

*A man who desires revenge should dig two graves.* Where had he heard that before?

*Do not seek revenge. The rotten fruits will fall by themselves.* And where had he also heard that?

How many dragons had he slain? Did *they* have families? Would someone be waiting endlessly for *them* to return home from wherever? Were any of them actually the ones who had done such horrible things to

Meili? Had any of them actually committed *any* crimes? Could he have possibly started a gang war, with each one of the Triad societies believing that someone from the other rival gangs murdered their members? What violence would now ensue?

Jian Hyui thought back again to Devon Stone's book, *The Fallen*, and all the revenge murders. He thought when he first read the book and had been inspired by it that the murders were justified. Now he wasn't so sure. Devon Stone had never answered his question regarding his *own* feelings about revenge killings being justified. Jian Hyui had not liked the fact that the heroine of that book did not survive. But perhaps there *was* a reason for that. Murderers should *not* get away with it. Should they? Could they? Would *he* get away unpunished? *Should* he?

*I am no better than any of the Triads* he thought.

He sat there as his sobbing slowly ceased and his breathing returned to normal. Five minutes went by. Then ten more. He stood up and went back out into the hallway. He thought about it for a moment and turned toward the door that led to the stairwell up to the rooftop.

His heart began pounding again as he slowly climbed the narrow spiral staircase.

*I may be going out on a limb here*, Devon Stone thought to himself.

"If," Devon began, as Jeremy Fleck simply sat and stared in disbelief at what had just transpired, "I can piece some information together, we, meaning you and me, can work together on this. I may have done you a major injustice. *But* I'll warn you, Jeremy Fleck, I still may be totally off base and you may have really pulled a slick one. Care for a smoke, by the way?"

Jian Hyui stepped out onto the gravel-topped rooftop and the heavy metal door slammed shut behind him. The storm clouds had parted, there was still just a hint of light in the sky and stars began to twinkle. A silver slice of a crescent new moon hung in the sky like the Cheshire cat's grin. He stood there breathing in the crisp fresh air. His mind cleared along with the weather.

He slowly walked toward the edge of the building. The edge where Meili had vanished. It seemed so long ago. He looked out across the narrow street and stared at Kowloon Walled City.

*I will never, ever step foot in that forbidden, foreboding hellhole again* he thought to himself. He stepped closer to the edge. And then even closer. He was feeling dizzy.

His imagination clicked on and he stared, now, down to the dirty ground five stories below. He imagined the loud singing of cicadas but it was too late in the season for that. They were gone. He saw a beautiful, lush green flower-filled garden where, in actuality, there was none. He smiled down at a beautiful young girl when, in actuality, there was no one there. She smiled back up at him and waved a small, precious hand. She brushed her long shiny black hair from across her face.

"Thank you!" she called up to him. "Thank you, my friend!"

He looked up to the sky, paused, and then looked back down to the dusty, barren, empty ground below. She had vanished once again but he still heard the cicadas singing.

He sighed as a single tear let loose from an eye and trickled down his check. He tasted its saltiness as it hit his lips.

He stepped back, then turned around and went back downstairs to his apartment.

By the time he awoke from his peaceful sleep a few hours later the sun was shining brightly through his dirty bedroom window. He had not had one solitary dream but he was positive that he still heard the cicadas singing.

In Chinese folklore, the cicada is an emblem of immortality and resurrection, and is also a symbol of eternal youth and happiness.

Billy Bennett was positive that he smelled smoke. He had been thoroughly engrossed in rereading one of Devon Stone's recent books, *Beacon Of Betrayal*, but had dozed off for a while. He thought he might have heard some raised voices coming from downstairs just a short time ago, but it was silent now. Maybe a little *too* silent. He was sure he sniffed the familiar aroma of cannabis. Now he was hungry, and slightly more than a little curious as to what was going on a couple floors below him.

And he had to go to the bathroom.

He carefully, quietly opened his bedroom door.

There was silence at first…and then some raucous laughing…and then the sounds of males giggling like little kids.

He slowly made his way down the staircase to the point where he could peek into the room where the sounds emanated.

*What in the hell is going on in there?* Billy Bennett thought.

A man Billy did not know was sitting eating what looked like a dish of vanilla ice cream. Devon Stone was about to take a bite out of what looked like a bright green apple. No, wait. That wasn't an apple. It was a green bell pepper.

Billy shook his head in disbelief.

Devon caught sight of him.

"Billy, Billy, Billy, my man!" Devon called. "Damn, I totally forgot I had you hidden away. Come join us. Things are turning out a lot differently than I had thought. Come on in. Here, I'll fix you a drink, and introduce you to my new friend. Want a smoke?"

Shortly after one-thirty A.M. a very tired Veronica Barron, thinking that everyone must surely be in bed by now, quietly unlocked the front door to Devon's house and stepped inside. The foyer was dark, but there was light coming from a room just down the hallway. She smelled the familiar aroma of cannabis, heard some loud male laughter, and saw Billy stagger out into the hall in front of her.

"What the hell is going on here?" she said out loud.

Billy Bennett had what looked like a loosely rolled joint dangling from his lips; he was wearing his trilby hat on backwards and he smiled when he saw her.

"Hi, toots!" he said with a silly grin on his face.

And he wasn't wearing any pants.

# 30

"*Toots?*" said Veronica. "Did you just call me *toots*? That's something your buddy Peyton would say. And where are your pants?"

Billy looked down at his boxers and at his hairy, muscular legs as his hat slid off his head and onto the floor.

"What? Hey, where are my pants?" he said looking confused. "It sure got hot in here, didn't it? Aren't you hot? Holy cow, it sure got hot. Wow, *you're* hot!"

Veronica shook her head and giggled.

"You're a mess, Billy. Drunk obviously, and stoned as well I have no doubt. And pantsless."

"It's all my fault," Devon Stone called out loudly in the room from which a high Billy Bennett had just stumbled. "I had him locked up but he escaped."

Devon laughed.

Veronica was afraid to ask.

She stepped into the room and was surprised to see an unfamiliar man sitting on the floor, cross-legged, eating a banana. Devon sat, slumped back in a big chair, peeling and then nibbling leaves from a head of cabbage.

"Dear, dear Veronica," called Devon, "Come in, come in! Please say hello to my new best friend, Jeremy Fleck. I thought he was rotten in

Denmark and killed his werewolf. He says he didn't. But, who knows? Maybe he *did*!"

Veronica's mouth hung open. Then she simply shook her head. *Some children should never be left alone unattended*, she thought.

Jeremy Fleck raised the half-eaten banana as if giving a toast.

"And you must be the reining queen of the London stage," he said only slightly slurring his words. "Can't wait to see your show, my dear, and see if you're any better at solving murders on stage than your stoned friend Stone is in real life."

Both he and Devon laughed as though that was the funniest thing ever spoken.

"Hey, *there* they are!" Billy exclaimed.

He had just seen where his pants had landed after he had discarded them an hour earlier.

"Don't bother putting them on, Billy," said Veronica with a slightly exasperated tone, sounding a bit like a mother scolding her naughty little boy. "It's obviously *way* past your bedtime. Get upstairs to our room. If you can manage the stairs, that is. Put on your jammies, brush your teeth and climb into bed. Nice meeting you, Jeremy. I think. I'm sure Devon will fill me in with all the vivid details about what went on here this evening when or *if* he finally comes back down to Earth."

"You're radishes, Veronica," Billy Bennett said drunkenly as he smiled at her and stumbled on the first step. He stopped. "Wait. I meant *ravishing*, Veronica." And he giggled. "Simply ravishing."

"I know, I know. Up ya go, cowboy!" she said pointing to the stairs, shaking her head and swatting him on his behind. "Up ya go. I swear, Billy Bennett, sometimes your shenanigans are enough to drive a saint insane."

Devon and Jeremy continued to talk, drink and smoke well into the early morning hours. Their conversation would probably have made no sense to anyone but them, but Veronica heard their unbridled laughter as she tried her best to go to sleep. A completely unexpected bond had formed between the two men. Too drunk and too high to even go out the front door, Devon offered Jeremy one of his remaining guest rooms and Jeremy readily accepted, falling asleep...or passing out as soon as he hit the bed.

Devon went to his own bedroom but lay awake for another hour with thoughts racing through his mind, his incredible memory spinning back in time. Wheels within wheels.

Devon, surprisingly alert, fixed a bountiful breakfast when he finally awoke later in the morning. Jeremy Fleck, in rumpled clothing, which he apparently had slept in, staggered, bleary-eyed, into the kitchen. Obviously Veronica and Billy would remain asleep and unseen for hours yet. The two men downed enough coffee to keep them awake for days, as their animated conversation dealt with all the facts, as they knew them. Devon was hoping that he wasn't mistaken. Jeremy, for his own reasons, was hoping that he was.

Devon Stone poured himself another cup of coffee, Jeremy Fleck declined, waving the pot away as Devon brought it toward his cup.

"I have this little nugget of an idea," Devon said after a few moments of quiet contemplation.

"A gold nugget...or fool's gold?" asked Jeremy with a snicker.

"We'll just have to see how it pans out, won't we? Pun intended. We'll find out shortly...one way or the other," Devon answered. "In any event, this is going to be one very busy and *very* long day. We shan't forget Veronica's big night tonight!"

Devon Stone's unfailingly exceptional memory had flashed back to the evening he received the strange package containing Samuel Fleck's manuscript and that ominous note. And to the young man who had delivered it.

He was now disturbed by his own inaction months ago when he had felt that something was not quite right about the situation. His instincts had warned him, yet he had let it pass. But there *had* been distractions. Lydia Hyui, for one, and her brother Jian. A trip to Hong Kong. The arrival of Veronica Barron. Not to mention trying to start, much less finish, his latest book. Excuses, excuses.

If he had checked out this unknown solicitor Blackstone right from the beginning, perhaps things would now be totally different. But he still had to make certain.

He reached for the telephone, making call after call for ninety minutes.

He then called his next-door neighbor Chester Davenport, and followed *that* call with one to Chester's friend Fiona Thayer to see if they, with their varied connections, could do some quick fact-finding on a couple certain individuals and possible connecting incidents.

The telephone calls were proving to be intriguing and extremely informative, to say the least. Devon was feeling even more confident that what he now was thinking was completely accurate. And *that* irritated him even further.

Finally he had one more call to make, one that could prove...or disprove the final part of his theory. It was barely past noon when he placed a call to his publishing house.

"Dartmouth Press," answered a sweet-sounding operator. "How may I direct your call?"

Devon was hoping that the woman, who he barely knew, wouldn't recognize his voice.

"Yes, good afternoon, ma'am," Devon responded, lying and trying to alter his voice a bit. "I've just gotten into town. I am trying to locate a friend from university and all I know is that he works for a publishing house. I've been calling all over. Would someone by the name of Jesse Thorndike be in your employ?"

"Well, this *is* your lucky day, sir," chirped the operator. "And a lucky phone call. Mr. Thorndike is one our newest editorial assistants. He's *such* a sweetheart. Would you like me to put you through to his line?"

"Oh, no thank you, miss," answered Devon with a huge grin. "Now that I know where he works, I would just *love* to pop in and surprise him. Please don't alert him. This is such good news!"

"Oh, I'm thrilled that I could be of help, Mr....?"

But Devon had hung up.

Jeremy Fleck had been listening and he perked up. He reacted with a quizzical look.

"Wait a minute. Now I'm *really* confused. So it was this Jesse Thorndike bloke who was the culprit all along, eh?"

"No, sir," answered Devon Stone. "I shall assume at this point that Jesse Thorndike, sweetheart though he may be, was just a totally innocent, unsuspecting courier."

Jeremy Fleck listened intently while Devon Stone explained the scenario as he saw it and what actions must take place now. He didn't want to believe Devon, but it appeared that certain facts were indisputable.

"How do you think he'll react?" asked Fleck.

Devon Stone shrugged his shoulders and slowly shook his head.

"People are unpredictable, Fleck. Desperate people even more so."

Forty-five minutes later, both Chester Davenport and Fiona Thayer called back to confirm what Devon had hypothesized.

And now they had work to do.

And quickly.

James Flynn stood, looking out of one his office windows as the rain had slowed the traffic ten stories below. He had a prestigious corner office and could view the streets in different directions. Car horns were honking and pedestrians were huddled under umbrellas. *Typical London weather*, he thought He glanced down at his appointment book lying open on his desk, and was slightly startled by his telephone ringing. One of his brand new authors wasn't due for another hour, yet the receptionist out front had just notified him that he had a visitor. She didn't say whom.

He walked down the hallway from his office and stopped in his tracks when he saw Devon Stone. He looked confused but he smiled.

"Devon, what an unexpected surprise to see you," Flynn said with outstretched hand. They shook hands and smiled pleasantly at each other. "I have a few moments before my next appointment. Some new young guy. His work looks promising. I wish you had called. What can I help you with?"

"I'd like to discuss a book with you, James," said Devon Stone with a broad smile.

"Outstanding!" said Flynn, still a bit confused. "Come back to my office. Maybe we can make this brief."

"Oh, it should only take a moment," said Devon Stone with a broad smile. "Well, maybe two."

James Flynn turned and walked back up the hall, ushering Devon back to his office passing dozens of framed covers from novels, several of them Devon Stone's and three of Samuel Fleck's. Devon took note of the fact that the three covers pertaining to Fleck's novels were of the first three successful ones.

Flynn told Stone to sit as he slowly closed the door.

"So, you have your new book in mind, Devon?" Flynn asked. "You've *finally* broken that dreaded writer's block?"

"Not really," Devon responded. "It's an old book."

James Flynn looked *really* confused now and cocked his head.

"But first, James, I have a question for *you*. Do you know of a solicitor Blackstone?"

A hesitation.

"Hmm, no, Devon, I do not. I have no idea who he is."

"Apparently no one else in London has, either, James. I was on the telephone calling law firms all around the city and its environs for more than an hour earlier today."

James Flynn began to fidget.

"Why? What has this Blackstone done?" Flynn asked, looking at Devon while shaking his head.

"Not a bloody thing if the bloke doesn't even exist," answered Devon. "I may or may not get back to this mysterious Blackstone in a minute, James, although I feel certain that he is totally fictitious. I also made several calls to your competitors. Other publishing houses. The old book, though, to which I was referring a few moments ago was one of *mine*. One of my earlier efforts. *Wheels Within Wheels*. Do you recall that one?"

"Well, don't be ridiculous, Devon, of course I do. Up until *The Fallen*, it had been your best seller."

"And one, my frightening memory tells me, that Samuel Fleck had *not* read prior to his...suicide."

"So?" asked an incredulous James Flynn. "How on earth would you even know that?"

"Call it coincidence or whatever you wish, James, but I was sitting here in this very office...in this very chair, for that matter, when I glanced at a copy of *Wheels Within Wheels* that you had your secretary bring into you while I was here."

James Flynn sat back, trying to remember the incident, and that particular time when Devon Stone had been in his office.

"That was, what, months ago?" Flynn asked, not knowing where this subject was going. "If *I* remember correctly, yes, Fleck had not read it and being that I was going to meet with him to discuss *his* latest book I thought I would take him a copy. I believe, now, that I may have even asked you to inscribe it. And then a day or so later the poor man committed suicide."

"Yes," said Devon, "that is correct. You *claimed* to have met with him at my favorite hangout, the Thorn Bush, right?"

"I imagine that's so, Devon. If you say so."

"Ah. But you *didn't* meet with him at the pub, did you, Flynn?"

James Flynn swallowed hard.

"I didn't think anything about it at the time you told me...really had no reason to do so," continued Devon. "I was too stunned by the news of his suicide to fully realize what you had actually just said. I should have paid closer attention, and I now regret that. But Fleck didn't like going to the Thorn Bush any more, as a matter of fact. He had been asked on several occasions to leave the premises because he had gotten a bit too rowdy and drunkenly obnoxious. It's one of the quieter, more refined pubs in the city. He also tried to get a bit too flirtatious with one of the barmen. I was with him on those occasions and it embarrassed him. He would *never* go there again, and told me that on more than one occasion. So I can't imagine him *ever* suggesting meeting you there. But then, *you* wouldn't know that, would you? Why didn't you just send the book to him via your private courier...young Mr. Thorndike?"

James Flynn, frowning, sat back in his chair and Devon Stone held his glare.

"What does Thorndike have to do with this, Stone? He's just a fucking editorial assistant, for Christ's sake. Damn it, man, you're confusing me!"

"I claim that *you* made a visit to Fleck's home. Maybe proposed as a nice friendly visit. Or not, I assume."

"How the hell would you even know *that*?" asked Flynn, shrugging his shoulders.

"We'll get to that in a minute," answered Devon. "Maybe that can be verified, so I must be patient."

"You've been reading *and* writing too many thrillers, Stone," quipped James Flynn, still befuddled, but shaken by this surprise visit from the author. "I'm not liking this behavior one bit. Are you playing some sort of twisted game with me here?"

"Someone *is* playing a game here, Flynn, but it sure as hell ain't me," said Devon as a grin began to creep across his face. "When you called to tell me about Fleck's suicide you mentioned that your relationship with him had become very tense and that your conversations were terse. I do believe you *were* being quite honest there. But not for the reason I originally thought. Extortion is a crime, James. Not nearly as serious as murder, but a crime nonetheless."

"Get to the point, will you, Stone?" said Flynn as he glanced down at his watch. "I have another appointment in ten minutes."

"The point is, Flynn," Devon said as he, too, glanced at his watch, "you were blackmailing Samuel Fleck and, unfortunately, ultimately ended up killing him."

James Flynn shot straight up out of his chair abruptly.

"Are out of your *fucking* mind!" he practically yelled, with flailing arms in the air.

"If someone has you by the balls, Flynn, you shouldn't be jumping up out of that seat so quickly. You can deny it until the cow jumps over the moon, James," Devon said as he sat back in his chair, crossing his legs, "but deadly facts are still…well, deadly facts. I never, *ever* would have thought you had a perfidious nature. You, of all people. I *will* say that you were quite shrewd as well as quite devious. Practicing what you publish, as it were. Obviously, somewhere along the line, you must have had some suspicion about my thoughts regarding the so-called suicide. So why not throw a little obfuscation into the works, eh? Try to throw my thoughts of Fleck's possible murder towards his estranged son. You certainly weren't thinking clearly. That inane ruse would have worked for only a while, James. Murder will out, as someone once said."

The telephone rang.

Devon Stone glanced at his watch again.

"Well, I'll be damned," he exclaimed. "Speaking of which…right on time. Your next appointment has just arrived. Sorry to tell you, though, it's not the one you were expecting."

# 31

The door to James Flynn's office burst open with his secretary yelling in the background "Sir...*sir!* Wait, please! You can't go in there!"

Devon Stone laughed raucously. Wasn't that the title of the mysterious, infamous last manuscript by Samuel Fleck?

"Brilliant! Isn't *that* ironic?" he said clapping his hands.

Jeremy Fleck stood in the doorway, folding his arms across his chest.

James Flynn sat back down in this chair and looked back and forth between the two men in his office. His face was flushed.

"James," said Jeremy Fleck, "you look as though you just discovered that you stepped in dog shit."

"You two are insane!" James Flynn said, trying to remain composed but doing a very poor job of it.

"No, we are *in sync*, James...not insane. We both know, now, that Samuel Fleck did *not* commit suicide. And we both know now who done him in, as that quaint expression goes."

James Flynn sat forward, elbows on his desk, staring at Devon Stone.

"Just how far do you think you're going with this asinine accusation, Stone?"

Devon Stone stared right back at his publisher. "I didn't come this far just to come this far, Flynn."

"Meaning?"

"Meaning that we *now* know that you blackmailed and then murdered poor Samuel Fleck. Probably because he was about to turn the tables on *you*."

"This is a fucking outrage, and I won't tolerate it! I have done nothing wrong. I am a totally innocent man. Get out, the both of you! I'll sue you both for slander. Or libel. Or both. You can't substantiate *anything* that you are standing there accusing me of," Flynn said, shaking his head and shrugging his shoulders.

Devon glanced quickly at Jeremy and Jeremy nodded, giving him the thumbs up gesture.

"Perhaps not," answered Devon Stone, also shrugging his shoulders. "But your accomplice can."

"And did," added Jeremy Fleck. "To the authorities. Not more than thirty minutes ago."

James Flynn slumped back in his chair. His balloon had just been pricked.

"You bastards! I'm calling my lawyer," he whimpered.

"Don't bother," responded Jeremy Fleck. "I advised your secretary to do just that as I breezed by her desk. I can assume that the next time your telephone rings it won't be to alert you regarding your *expected* appointment."

And with that, Devon and Jeremy left Flynn's office, quietly closing the door behind them.

Devon Stone and Jeremy Fleck went back out through the lobby and reached for the door just as it was opening. A nicely dressed fresh-faced young man, probably in his mid-twenties entered, smiled at the men and stepped aside.

"Might you be the new author who's coming for a meeting with James Flynn?" asked Jeremy Fleck.

"Why, yes, sir, I sure am," said the man with a huge, proud smile on his face.

"I hate to tell you, lad," said Devon Stone, *trying* his best to look despondent, "but Mr. Flynn won't be able to keep that appointment."

"I'm fairly certain that he'll be booked up...probably for years to come," laughed Jeremy Fleck.

Both men left the office and walked, now, in somber silence toward the elevators. Each with contrasting and conflicting thoughts.

Devon Stone and Jeremy Fleck shared a cab with the first stop to drop Jeremy off at his father's house. The men rode in silence for the first half of the ride. Each looking out of the rain-swept windows as the streets of London went by. The wet, traffic-clogged streets slowed the ride that each hoped would end soon. Devon had writing to do. The brick wall securing his writer's block had crumbled. Jeremy had his father's affairs to finally settle and then return to Hong Kong.

But, more importantly and more immediate, later that evening they would be heading to the theater. Veronica Barron's opening night had finally arrived and each man was hoping for a pleasant diversion from what had just transpired.

Devon was feeling regretful towards the man sitting by his side. The one he had continually accused of murdering his father. But there was another reason.

"Jeremy," Devon said, finally breaking the uncomfortable silence, "I can't imagine how you might be feeling at the moment."

Jeremy Fleck slowly turned his head toward Devon. His eyes were glassy and reddened. He gave Devon a wan smile along with a gentle shrug of his shoulders.

"Crestfallen would be a good word to start with. I don't know how I could have been *so* foolish," he said with a catch in his voice. "I never, *ever* suspected a thing. I was completely taken in. I was as positive that my father's death was a suicide as much as *you* were positive that it was murder. The bloody authorities seemed to have forgotten about the case entirely. God only knows how long they had been planning this ruse. It was so easy, I guess, with me being a world away in Hong Kong."

Devon placed a friendly, reassuring hand on Jeremy's knee and squeezed it gently.

Jeremy turned his head again toward the window and inhaled deeply, releasing a loud sigh.

"How long did it take? I mean, the confession," asked Devon. "Once you had stated the facts and figures that you and I uncovered."

"Blimey! You mean after the weeping and wailing, gnashing of teeth... and eventual name calling?" answered Jeremy, "Actually not as long as I had thought. Jesus, I never *heard* such words! Never once was there a denial, though, unlike with Flynn back there."

"Did you love her?" asked Devon.

"I thought I might have. At one time. It was fun for a while, but she was often remote. Ha! And I was more often *really* remote. By thousands of miles. For Christ's sake, at my age I should have known better. I guess I was just tired of being alone. Who knows, now, with all the deceptions, if Beth Barnes is even her real name?"

*Three hours and forty-five minutes earlier...*

After his long conversation and revelations discovered with Devon Stone, Jeremy Fleck rushed back to his late father's house, hoping that Beth Barnes was still there. At this point, she hadn't suspected that anything was amiss.

At the same time, Devon Stone placed a call to his friend Agatha Christie. Following a short but informative conversation, Devon placed two other telephone calls; one to Jeremy Fleck, hoping that, by now, Jeremy had made it back to his father's house.

"Mr. Fleck's residence," Beth Barnes said.

"Ah, good, Miss Barnes," answered Devon, "I was hoping that someone was still there and the place hadn't been locked up yet. Is Jeremy there, by any chance? I really need to speak to him about an urgent matter. This is Devon Stone, by the way."

"No, Mr. Stone, I'm sorry he's not here at the moment. I have no idea...oh, wait. I hear the front door opening. I can assume that it's Mr. Fleck. I hope it is anyway, and not some intruder." And she gave a nervous little laugh.

"For your sake, Miss Barnes, I, too, hope it's not an intruder. One can never be too safe these days, can one?"

Beth Barnes couldn't see that Devon Stone had a huge grin on his face.

Devon heard some conversation in the background, footfall on hardwood flooring, and then the receiver was picked up.

"Well, Devon? What did you discover?" Jeremy Fleck asked.

"I'm glad you spoke to the medical examiners when you did. Obviously I had no legal right or reason to do so at the time. But *you* certainly did. That information helped us tremendously. I guess we can now see why there was an open verdict. As you may know, my friend Miss Christie is an expert on poisons. Homicide detectives have called upon her expertise on several occasions."

"Yes, Devon, I know that quite well. And?"

"Thallium, Jeremy, is tasteless and odorless. Murderers have often used it because it's sometimes difficult to detect. Actually, Dame Agatha has used it in one of her books."

"Really," responded Jeremy. "Interesting. But how did they get it, you imagine?"

"Well…for one thing, it's used as rat poison, Jeremy."

"Dear, God!" gasped Jeremy Fleck.

"Now is the time, my friend, for a nice long chat with that sweet young thing who you have probably been bedding. Who knows, *you* may have been a potential target as well. It could have easily been set up to look like a suicide. You know? Guilt-stricken son murdered his father and then ended it all when the law became suspicious."

"Jesus Christ," muttered Jeremy.

"Better get with her quickly, Jeremy. I'm betting on her crumbling and confessing as soon as you confront her. I took the liberty of contacting a homicide detective I've known for some time. I called him just before I called you now. He should be at your place within the hour. Make it as fast as you can, and plan to meet me at Flynn's office in two hours if you can."

*Six months earlier…at the home of Samuel Fleck*

"Damn it to hell, I've lied about my life long enough, James," shouted Samuel Fleck as he paced back and forth in front of James Flynn. "I should never have caved into your villainous scheme right from the start. My mind is unraveling and the guilt, to say nothing of the remorse, is now too much to take. I simply can't take this subterfuge any longer and I will not be bullied into any further blackmail from you. I've paid enough. And enough is enough! Enough is too much. You're a fucking bastard. Through and through. My lying is over. I'll confess my charade to the press, to my faithful readers if I have any left…to my poor son…to the whole fucking world. But you'll not be getting another shilling from me. And I just might expose *you* for what you really are."

James Flynn stood silently for a moment. He had arrived ten minutes earlier carrying a small sack, which he still held. He smiled at Beth Barnes who was also in the room.

"You are *absolutely* right, Samuel," he finally spoke, trying his best to sound remorseful. "I don't know what I must have been thinking at the time. I've made a horrible mess of this situation and I now regret what I've been doing to you. I shall return all the money you've paid to me. I never, ever should have done this to you. Maybe I was just desperate at the time. Who knows what was going through my mind? Please. Let's turn back the clock and reset our friendship. Look, I brought this nice expensive wine as a peace offering to you. Please accept it along with my profound apologies."

James Flynn opened the sack that he had been holding and pulled out a bottle of 1947 Cheval Blanc, once considered the best Bordeaux ever made.

Samuel Fleck stopped pacing and stood firm, folding his arms across his chest. He glanced at the wine and glowered at James Flynn.

"Come on, Fleck," said Flynn with feigned good humor. "Yes, I've committed a detestable crime and I truly regret it. I shall probably rot in hell for it and justifiably. But I shall not betray your trust any further. Ever again. That's my solemn promise. I'll not reveal to anyone what you have done in the past. Please. Please, Samuel. Let's put all of this nastiness behind us, and let's toast to our renewed friendship."

Samuel Fleck still just stared at James Flynn; his temper had still not receded.

"I don't mean to be presumptuous," Flynn said, "but Miss Barnes maybe you'd be kind enough to uncork this and bring us each a nice glass of wine?"

Beth Barnes took both the bottle and the sack from James Flynn and went out to the kitchen.

Samuel Fleck sat down in his comfortable easy chair, still scowling at his deceitful publisher.

"One drink and you're gone, Flynn," said Samuel Fleck. "Out of my house and out of my life. I'll find another publisher, but you can keep your fucking, bloody money. *My* money. I want nothing more to do with this episode of my life. And I'm going to make everything right with my poor son once again. I'm hoping that he'll forgive me."

Beth Barnes entered the room carrying two glasses of red wine. She smiled sweetly as she handed one to Fleck and then nodded to Flynn as she handed one to him.

"Cheers, Samuel," said James Flynn as he raised his glass in a toast and smiled.

"Up yours, Flynn," answered Samuel Fleck as he raised his glass to his lips and drank.

*Present day, present time*

Less than five minutes after Devon and Jeremy had left the premises, James Flynn's now-distraught secretary escorted the two uniformed Bobbies and the homicide detective into his office. They found that it was empty. A cold, wet breeze was blowing in from an open office window. There was a distant rumble from a rare thunderstorm and an unusually loud commotion was heard coming from down on the street...ten stories below.

# 32

November 11, 1955
9:30 P.M. - Opening Night: *"Nick & Nora!"*

The first act curtain had just descended as the main character Nora Charles (Veronica Barron, still beautiful but almost unrecognizable in a brunette wig done in a 1940s bob) brings down the house with a hilarious, double entendre-loaded parody of a torch song called *I Just Got Pinched In The Astor Bar!*

Billy Bennett's hands were sore from clapping so hard. Sitting beside him Jeremy Fleck, Devon Stone and Lydia Hyui had tears streaming down their cheeks from laughing so hard. Chester Davenport and his friend Fiona Thayer were sitting directly behind them.

"By Jove, Stone," Chester said as he leaned forward, tapping Devon on his shoulder. "I thought you detested musicals."

Devon, still laughing, answered, "I do believe that Veronica may have just changed my mind." *And it was a pleasant change of pace from the* real *murder we just solved*, Devon thought to himself as he glanced at Jeremy Fleck. "Who knew murder could be so much fun?"

"Maybe your *next* book, Devon," Jeremy Fleck added, "should be all singing, all dancing!"

The audience was abuzz as the lights came up and, based upon the reaction from the first act alone, the show would be an enormous hit.

But that would soon present a problem.

Two hours later, Nick and Nora Charles had solved not one, but *three* murders, stopped the show cold with a rousing, foot-stomping, roof-raising song and dance, *That Last Martini,* and sent the theater critics scrambling for their thesauruses to find enough superlatives to be used in their respective reviews.

After battling the crowds trying the leave the theater and getting taxicabs, Devon, Lydia, Jeremy, Chester, and Fiona headed to their reserved table in the upstairs private dining room at The Ivy, a favored late-night dining spot in Covent Garden dating back to 1917. Billy was waiting outside the theater for Veronica and would soon join them.

Making a very quick and brief appearance at the impromptu cast celebration backstage, Veronica located Billy and finally arrived at The Ivy. By this time, the group was into their second round of drinks and they all were laughing and chattering like a flock of kookaburras. They quickly stood in unison, though, when Veronica was escorted into the room and happily applauded her loudly. Billy proudly stepped back and smiled as his wife drank in the adulation.

"Oh, please," Veronica said, "Sit, sit, sit. Evidently I may be way behind you with the drinks and I simply *must* catch up!"

"With a martini?" quipped Devon Stone.

"With several, please," was Veronica's quick response.

Several martinis later and luscious dinners all around, the conversation segued from musical murders into a real-life murder.

"Oh, my gosh!" exclaimed Veronica Barron loudly. "With all the long days and late night rehearsals I totally forgot all about that suicide thing you were thinking about, Devon. Well? Was it *really* suicide or were you correct about it being a murder? Have I totally missed out on all the excitement? If there *had* been any!"

Chester Davenport glanced at Fiona Thayer and then leaned forward, elbows on the table.

"Yes, Devon," he said with a smile. "Please *do* fill us in. Did the information that dear Fiona here and I gave you pan out?"

He already knew the answer.

"Wait," said Billy Bennett with a confused look on his face. "I seem to remember something about a suicide. Was there a murder, *too*? Did I miss something?"

Veronica Barron laughed, throwing her head back.

"I think, dearest Billy," she finally said, "a few nights ago you had perhaps too much to drink and seriously too much of something to smoke. And, to top it off, you were caught with your pants down."

Devon Stone and Jeremy Fleck laughed hysterically. Chester Davenport and Fiona Thayer simply looked at each other and shrugged their shoulders.

"Go ahead, Stone," said Jeremy Fleck. "You solved the mystery, my friend, you may as well tell the story. I'm sure it will work its way into a book of yours in the near future. If you can find a new trustworthy publisher, that is."

Devon Stone chuckled and rolled his eyes.

"But this should be *Veronica's* night tonight, my friends," he said. "We should all be celebrating her successful return to the London stage, not talking about a real-life murder plot."

"That's fine," Veronica said, "and I certainly appreciate that, but no dice. I want to hear about the resolution to this situation. Darn it, I never even had a chance to get involved. Were you ever in any danger, Devon?"

"Well," he said with a chuckle as he quickly glanced at Jeremy Fleck. "For a while there, I thought that Fleck, here, might beat me senseless with a bottle of my best gin. But he passed out first."

"Devon," Lydia Hyui interjected quickly. "Now you're just being silly. Don't stall for time. I *do* know that you two, you and Jeremy, were at odds up until a night or so ago. Were you right?"

He hesitated and then took in a deep breath and cleared his throat.

"I was right," he began, "and I was wrong. I was right about the situation *not* being a suicide. I was wrong in thinking that it was patricide."

"*Now* I remember! I know what *that* is!" interrupted Billy Bennett proudly. "Another word for murder, right?"

Devon laughed.

"Yes, for the longest time I was convinced that Jeremy here...poor Jeremy, had killed his father."

"Oh, for the love of God, cut to the chase, Devon," blurted Fiona Thayer. "We all know the *first* part. Get to the juicy part."

Devon downed his martini and signaled the waiter for another.

"All right, then," he began once more. "Samuel Fleck's part-time house keeper, Beth Barnes, was a fraud. Well, she was simply posing as a housekeeper. She had been a copy editor at a less than reputable publishing house for several years. One of the publishing concerns where Samuel had submitted his first disastrous manuscripts. She had been seriously surprised when *Open Verdict*, Fleck's first bestseller was published by Dartmouth, a rival firm. She noticed that his writing style had improved tremendously and was, at that time, very impressed. That book was followed by two more bestsellers. Ah, but then, came book number four. Awful book number four."

Devon stopped to take a sip from his latest martini. The others in the group followed suit. Veronica was transfixed.

"Book number four was followed by books five and six, each one worse than the one before. Frankly, I don't even know how they got published. Dear, sweet far-from-innocent Beth Barnes...*astute* Beth Barnes recognized that the writing style was exactly the same as those first manuscripts that had been rejected by her firm. Sooooo...she met with Fleck's latest publisher, James Flynn, taking one of those earlier manuscripts with her."

"Oh, no," interrupted Veronica. "I have a feeling I know where this is going."

"Do you have a song and dance to go along with that feeling, Veronica?" snickered Jeremy Fleck. "Was that a cue for the orchestra?"

"I don't know you well enough, Jeremy, to call you a smartass. But you're a smartass, aren't you?" Veronica retorted.

"Well played, Veronica. Well played," Jeremy said in response. "Okay, Devon, you're a great storyteller but you're making this long story even longer. Let me jump in here."

"Be my guest," laughed Devon Stone.

"Thanks, here, to Chester and Fiona for quickly ferreting out some sordid details. The honorable...and I use the term strictly tongue in cheek...publisher James Flynn was having a *wee* bit of a financial problem, to say the least. His wife was taking him to the cleaners in her extremely nasty but lucrative divorce settlement after catching him in flagrante delicto, believe it or not. So he and Barnes plotted a scheme. He knew that my father needed a part-time housekeeper. She, having recently left her employ at the publishing house, played the role perfectly. Not unlike you, Miss Barron. But without all the singing and dancing. Beth Barnes was keeping tabs on Father while James Flynn struck him with a threat of disclosure to the reading public. Blackmail, plain and simple. And she also played *me* like a fool, coming on to me in the most beguiling, but ultimately fraudulent, of ways."

Jeremy Fleck took a brief pause.

"This is certainly going to be a memorable night for all of us," he said with a wistful smile.

"To throw a bit of confusion into the mess," Devon interjected, "Flynn was a bit wary about my thoughts, so he sent one of Samuel's old manuscripts to me, with his young editorial assistant as an unsuspecting courier. Supposedly it was sent from Samuel's solicitor. A non-existent one, to boot! He wrote a note from the grave, so to speak, trying to make me believe that Samuel suspected his son of trying to get rid of him. The two different handwriting styles stuck in my mind until I confronted Jeremy about it."

All of a sudden, Devon Stone glanced around the room and noticed that half a dozen waiters were standing off to the side, whispering to each other and listening intently with eyes glued to the table. A couple of them had their arms folded across their chests.

"Oh, my word, we're so sorry, lads," Devon said abruptly as he looked at his watch. "We're chattering on and on and I'll bet you're waiting to clean up the place and close out, aren't you? We've been rude and inconsiderate. It must now be *way* past closing time. We're keeping you so late! I apologize."

"No, no, not at all, sir," said the spokesman for the waiters. "You all are the most *fascinating* guests we've had here in years. This story is better than anything we've seen on the telly. We're in agreement here and we can't *wait* to see how all this turns out. Stay until dawn, if you must!"

The table erupted in gales of laughter.

Chester Davenport raised a cup of coffee, shaking his head.

"Good lord, if you two gents don't pick up the bloody pace we *will* be here until dawn!" he said.

"Right," said Jeremy Fleck. "I agree. In her tearful, pitiful confession, Beth Barnes stated that my father, after well over a year of paying out, became irate and was about to turn the tables and alert the authorities about Flynn's blackmail. He no longer cared about his reputation. He was fed up with all the deceit, evidently. That's when blackmail suddenly became murder. Flynn had come to the house to fake an apology and they argued. Flynn had brought a bottle of wine, supposedly as a peace offering, knowing how much my father loved a good wine. He had brought something else as well. Beth Barnes knew exactly what to do at that point. She and Flynn had discussed this earlier. Father was then poisoned unknowingly. As he slowly died they propped him up in his easy chair and Flynn placed one of Devon's books on his lap making it appear as though he had been casually reading it before poisoning himself. Beth Barnes simply rinsed out Flynn's wine glass, put it away in its proper cabinet, and then threw an empty medicine bottle on the floor beneath my father's chair to further confound the authorities. The deed was done. The end."

Jeremy Fleck stood up to take a bow.

The waiters applauded.

"Well, this has been one hell of a day, hasn't it? Let us finish up here, friends," said Devon Stone. "We shall let the waiters do their jobs in peace and quiet so they can finally go home to their families and let's head for our *own* homes, late though it may be."

The meal was finished, Devon Stone paid the bill and, as they left, each of the group graciously shook hands with the waiters, an uncharacteristic move for restaurant diners. Waiting to be the last one to leave the dining room, Devon, with a wink, discretely handed each one of the eavesdropping but patient waiters a £10 note.

As satisfied as he was regarding the solving of the murder/suicide situation, Devon Stone was certain that the episode wasn't entirely resolved. He felt as though there was still a missing piece of the puzzle. And that missing piece somehow involved Lydia Hyui's brother, Jian. Jeremy Fleck was holding back. He *must* have known about his father's infatuation.

Devon was a bit surprised that Lydia hadn't asked Jeremy about it during dinner. Another private meeting with Jeremy Fleck was in order.

As euphoric as she was regarding the enthusiastic reception to the opening night performance, Veronica Barron had a piece of news to impart and was extremely apprehensive as to how it would be received.

Thirty minutes later, as they were all exiting their respective taxicabs in front of his home, Devon Stone happened to glance up at his front door. There was a lone figure sitting on the top step in the darkness.

*What now?* he thought.

# 33

The person, still in the shadows, slowly stood up as Devon Stone cautiously started up the steps to his house. Not knowing what to expect, Devon turned, telling the others to wait there on the sidewalk.

"My flight was delayed," Peyton Chase called out as he stood up. "Sorry I missed the party."

Hearing his voice, Veronica Barron ran up the stairs, nearly tripping over his duffle bag, giving him a tight embrace and kissed him on the cheek.

Billy Bennett ran up the steps close behind, shaking Peyton's hand.

"Oh, buddy, are we glad to see you!" he said. "Just wait until you hear what you've missed."

Chester Davenport turned to call up to Devon.

"Fiona and I are calling it a night, old friend. Too much excitement and all that crap, you know? Cheers to your roaring success, Veronica!"

Fiona winked and waved at Devon as she and Chester headed up the steps to his house next door.

"Well, come on in, now that Peyton is finally here," said Devon. "I know that it's quite late, but I've been chilling a wonderful 1907 Heidsieck

Champagne just for tonight's occasion, Veronica. Bravo, young lady. Bravo!"

Peyton Chase was introduced to both Jeremy Fleck and Lydia Hyui as Devon popped the cork on the first bottle of champagne. Billy and Veronica, chattering like magpies, brought Peyton up to speed on the murder/suicide situation albeit the *Reader's Digest* condensed version. And then Billy and Lydia bombarded poor Peyton with what he had missed earlier in the evening at the theater.

"Whoa, whoa, whoa," Peyton said laughing and holding up his hands as if in surrender. "I don't know if my mind can handle all this stuff so late in the night. Without a drink first, that is!"

"Perfect timing, young man," snickered Devon Stone as he passed around the filled fluted glasses. "Congratulations, again, Veronica. You and your show are simply fabulous, I must admit. You changed my mind about musicals. Well, as long as there might be a murder or two in them."

They all raised their glasses in a toast.

"I predict a long, long run," said Lydia Hyui. "I can't believe that it's scheduled for such a limited run of only three months, as you told us."

The expression on Veronica's face suddenly changed.

And Billy Bennett noticed it.

"What's the matter, Ronnie?" he asked. "What is it?"

All faces turned to Veronica.

"Wellllll," she said sheepishly. "Here's the situation. Maybe Billy and I should be discussing this in private."

"I repeat, Ronnie. What's the matter?"

Veronica Barron cleared her throat and took a sip of her champagne.

"Yes, the reception from the audience was overwhelming," she began. "Actually better here in London than it was on Broadway. I guess the simple rewrites and additional songs helped tremendously. All of us backstage relished the cheers and applause. We *live* for that kind of adulation."

"You're stalling, Veronica!" Billy Bennett blurted.

"Uh, oh…it's *Veronica* now, is it?" Veronica said weakly. "Okay. Here's the deal. The producers rushed backstage after the performance to tell us. They felt sure that we were going to have a great big hit on our hands and they wanted to surprise us right after the opening. It was all planned even before the actual opening night. They have extended the run for a year… possibly two, if ticket sales continue to surge as they expect them to do."

All faces then turned to Billy.

"You're going to be here in London for a whole *year*?" he said. "Ronnie, I really don't want to spoil the excitement from this evening. I am so proud of you I can't stand it. But, holy cow, a *year*?…possibly two? You know that I love you more than anything, but what the fuck?"

"Well, in that case," said Devon Stone, trying to lighten the mood, "I just may have to start charging rent!"

"Perhaps I shouldn't barge in here, Veronica," Jeremy Fleck added, "but it would seem to me that you originally probably signed a contract for a three-month run of the show. Unless there were clauses in that contract pertaining to a potential extension, then the producers can't arbitrarily extend the run without getting new contracts from their stars. In any event, you need to contact your agent in the morning."

Lydia Hyui shook her head and gave Veronica a sympathetic, knowing nod.

"Tough choice, isn't it, dear?" Lydia said. "A long, successful run or matrimonial harmony."

Peyton Chase threw his head back in laughter.

"I'm stayin' outta this one, kiddos," he said. "Fight nice!"

"Right. And on *that* happy note," Jeremy Fleck said, "this has been one hell of a day. A long, long, too long of a day. I'm going home…well, Father's home…to nurse my emotional wounds. I'll be back and forth over the next weeks between here and Hong Kong. Lydia, whenever you might be visiting Hong Kong again, let's meet for drinks. I'm sure we each know some great pubs."

"Oh, that would be wonderful, Jeremy," she responded. "Let's do. Then I could introduce you to my brother. I'm sure he'd be *thrilled* to meet you!"

*I'm sure thrilled isn't quite the right word*, thought Devon Stone.

As Devon escorted Jeremy Fleck to the front door, Jeremy leaned in and whispered into Devon's ear.

"Let's *you* and me meet at the Thorn Bush tomorrow evening, shall we? No poison involved, though. There are some things I know about her brother that may not sit too well with her. I'm fairly certain that it would upset her greatly."

181

Devon smiled and nodded.

"See you at eight, then?" he said as Jeremy stepped out the door.

"Eight it is, then," was the response. "Be prepared."

*Jian Hyui…man of mystery and surprises…what have you done?* Devon Stone thought to himself as he slowly closed the door.

Lydia Hyui was up early and out of the house by nine. She had to go home, change her clothes and then had a shop to open.

Veronica Barron was up and out of the house by ten, headed to the theater, ready to call her agent regarding the touchy situation regarding the show and her contract. She was well aware that prompt negotiations were in order.

Both Billy Bennett and Peyton Chase were up and out of the house by eleven to quickly see the sights before they each headed to their respective late afternoon flights to take them back to the States.

Devon Stone breathed in the absolute silence of his empty house. And he smiled. He walked up from his kitchen, cup of hot coffee in his hand, and headed to his office. He was totally naked.

*Haven't been able to do this in way too long*, he thought to himself as he snickered. *Shame on me!*

A few minutes later, after at least putting on a pair of boxers, Devon was playing his typewriter like a crazed man on a Steinway, with earthy, woody, sweet smelling smoke swirling around his head. Ideas were flowing like drinks at an open-bar wedding.

He never realized, at that moment, that what he would soon learn from Jeremy Fleck in a few short hours would change the whole direction and plot of his latest book.

# 34

Devon Stone and Jeremy Fleck, now good friends for life, sat in a quiet corner booth at the Thorn Bush enjoying the fact that their contentious beginnings in the week before were now resolved and past history.

"I hesitate to ask," said Jeremy Fleck after sipping his preferred martini, "what happened with Veronica's delicate situation with her husband?"

"As in all successful marriages...*ha!* Like I would even know anything about that! A compromise has been struck. Yes, she contacted her agent. She was familiar, indeed, with the original contract. While there actually *was* a clause in the original contract regarding an extension, it was to be negotiable. A new contract needs to be signed. She and Billy reached an agreement. That all-important compromise, as I said. Veronica has agreed to stay with the show for a six-month run *only*. No longer than that. No exceptions. No extensions. She will be granted two one-week vacations during that time. I assume she'll fly back to the States to coddle Billy for a few days during those times off."

"I shall not be selling my father's house here in London," said Jeremy Fleck. "At least not within this year, anyway. Veronica is free to use that place as her residence for the next six months so she can get out from under your nose. Needless to say, there will be no housekeeper involved."

"Very generous on your part, lad," responded Devon with a chuckle.

"I shall make her aware of your offer. Yes, actually, I *should* like to get my privacy back."

They each downed their drinks and signaled to Toby, the barman, for another.

"*Now*, Jeremy, let me have the tidbit that I know you've been holding back regarding Jian Hyui."

Their new drinks were delivered to the table as Jeremy Fleck took a deep breath.

"First and foremost," he said, as he looked around to make sure no one was within hearing distance. He leaned forward and whispered, "I have a rather startling, potentially blood-curdling confession to make."

*Oh, no,* thought Devon Stone as a chill went up his spine, *have I really been wrong about this bloke all along?*

Jeremy Fleck cleared his throat and a strange look came across his face. A look of apprehension? Or was it a look of guilt?

"Devon, I *am* a murderer. I *have* killed another man. Fairly recently. Shot the bastard in the head."

Devon Stone sat back, almost slamming his drink down on the table, splattering a bit of it, and glared at Jeremy Fleck. *What the fuck?* he thought.

"Hear me out, Devon, before you judge. You, yourself, have written about justifiable murders, haven't you? In *The Fallen*, if I remember correctly."

"Bloody hell, why does that blasted book keep popping up?" exclaimed Devon shaking his head. "I wish to hell that I'd never written the fucking thing now."

"And I misled you and Lydia, Devon, when I sort of insinuated that I wasn't aware of her brother."

"All right, Fleck, tell me something I *don't* know," Devon said, staring right into Fleck's eyes.

"I have kept tabs on my poor father for years. He was never aware of it. I was always cautious and surreptitious about my doings. Actually, I did *not* know about Jian Hyui until Father showed up in Hong Kong. Then I started keeping a watchful eye on *him*, meaning Jian. It was fortunate that I did. It saved *him* from being murdered."

"Do tell," said Devon Stone, now leaning on his elbows and sitting forward. "I thought that solving *one* murder this week would be sufficient. Your story seems to be proving otherwise. Go on."

"I already told you that I'm a journalist. I'm especially intrigued by the crime…and, believe me, there's plenty of that that goes on in Hong Kong."

The pub began to fill up and the noise level was increasing, causing the two men to lean in closer to each other on the table.

"There was a particular violent criminal that had attracted the attention of law enforcement…and me. Jian Hyui had also drawn the attention of this miscreant. And in the most unexpected of ways. Zhāng Wěi, also known as Qiang, was a member of one of the notorious Triad societies. They are well known for their codes of secrecy. Zhāng Wěi had a secret, all right. He was queer and lusted after Jian Hyui. Jian Hyui thwarted the lustful attempts, from what I had observed. This threw up a red flag in my mind and, rather than keeping an eye on Father while he was in town, I followed Jian hoping to be able to protect him in some way. Of course, at this point, I knew that my father had certain…umm…feelings for Lydia's brother."

By this time, Devon Stone was mesmerized. And started taking mental notes.

"Although it is strictly forbidden in Hong Kong, at that time I carried a secret pistol, mainly for my own protection when I was out and about in not the best of places. One fateful morning, I followed Jian onto the Star ferry. I saw that someone else had also followed Jian. I was shocked to see, even from a distance, that Zhāng Wěi slowly pulled something from his jacket and it appeared that he was about to attack Jian. It could have been a knife…or a gun…or another weapon of some sort. I just knew that an attack was about to happen right there on the boat. I reacted the only way I could. Granted, it was knee-jerk reaction. I suddenly shot the man from behind, blowing off half his head and causing a near riot and panic on the boat."

Devon was stunned, to say the least. He sat back and downed his drink.

"That was one hell of a risk you were taking there," Devon said, taken aback. "It could have turned tragic had you missed."

"What I did was beyond morally questionable and, if I even believed in such things, I should probably end up in hell. Or prison. But, no, Devon, I did not take an unnecessary, dangerous risk in shooting the man. I proudly wore the Marksman Badge for three years while serving in the British army. It was an easy shot. He was a ruthless murderer and was just about to commit another murder right there on the ferry. I was sure of it. With the ensuing panic aboard the vessel, no one paid any attention to me. Basically, I was almost invisible."

"And what was Hyui's reaction to this murder?" asked Devon Stone. "What happened after that?"

Jeremy Fleck sat back and became pensive.

"To shelter Lydia's…hmmm…peace of mind, you might want to discuss *that* with Jian in private somehow. I don't know why, but Jian Hyui seemed to go on a violent trek through the notorious Kowloon Walled City every once in a while soon thereafter. Late at night. I'll save the explanations for those said forays for you to discover from Jian. He and I have spoken about this situation at length. You may want to let him know that you and I have also discussed this to some degree. He may be very reluctant to discuss it with you. Then again, maybe not. He has met you. He is very fond of you. Use your persuasive wiles, Devon. You're very good at that! But I've observed that he seems to have become even more reclusive. Frankly, he probably needs years of therapy to help him get beyond what he did and where his mind is now. I think that his mind is in a very dark place at the moment. Who knows what might transpire?"

"What in the bloody hell?" said Devon with mouth agape. "So…you *are* a murderer. And you're telling me that apparently *Jian Hyui* is also a murderer. What next?"

Jeremy Fleck sat back with a wide smile on his face. A Cheshire cat kind of smile.

"So now we know something about each other that we don't wish to be divulged to the unsuspecting public…or the law, don't we?" asked Jeremy Fleck

That statement confused Devon Stone.

"I don't understand, Fleck. What could you possibly know about me that should remain secret? My life is an open book. A best seller."

Jeremy Fleck cleared his throat, sighed, leaned forward and looked Devon in the eye.

"We are *both* assassins…murderers," he whispered, looking around to make certain no one could hear them. "You and me. Or is it you and I?"

"I *write* about them, Fleck, I don't commit them."

"But I beg to differ with you, Mr. Stone. Don't be alarmed. I shall keep your murders secret if you promise to keep what I just told *you* a secret as well. Gentleman's honor."

"You have me at a disadvantage, Fleck. Please elaborate."

"Oh, please, Stone. Don't be coy. Your murders *were* justified in my book, no pun intended. Remember, I'm a journalist and a writer. A little over a year ago I was doing some research for a book I intend to write. One that I've already started, actually. A book about World War Two. I learned about some unusual heroics that took place during the war, perhaps even turning the tide in some instances. I interviewed a beautiful young Russian actress whose sister was murdered soon after the war. Her sister was one of the now-famous Night Witches of the Soviet army."

Devon Stone sat back in his seat.

"You interviewed Anoushka Markarova," he said. It was a statement, not a question.

Jeremy Fleck nodded.

"Your actions, and those of your little group of friends were commendable, to say the least, Mr. Stone. Illegal? Oh, beyond a shadow of a doubt, but commendable nonetheless. Justifiable homicide?" Fleck shrugged his shoulders. "I'm not a lawyer, just a journalist. Certain incriminating parts of that interview will never see the light of day. I made *that* solemn promise to Miss Markarova. I *will*, however, use the information I garnered from Miss Markarova in that book whenever I get around to finishing it…and under my *own* name this time. It should be very interesting reading, wouldn't you agree? Of course, just for fun I shall build some romance along with a modicum of sex into the story. I understand that one of your American friends got very…hmmm…how should I put this? Very close to Anoushka. But everything will be purely fictitious. Well, up to a point, anyway."

Devon Stone took another sip from his drink and smiled as he thought about the cocky, wisecracking Peyton Chase, and wondered what his intentions were for the beautiful Anoushka. He *did* know that the cocky, wisecracking Peyton Chase was smitten and was acting like a lovesick puppy dog. Ah, the problems of a long distance love affair. But that was not any of Devon Stone's concerns. He, also, had a book to finish. And someone he most definitely needed to speak with in Hong Kong.

"Are you afraid of anything, Devon?" asked Jeremy Fleck. A question out of the blue.

"I'm afraid of running out of ideas," Devon answered after a moment's thought. "I'm afraid of running out of time." A brief pause. "I'm afraid of running out of gin."

Jeremy Fleck chuckled.

"And you, Jeremy?"

"In this crazy, out-of-control world? I'm afraid of what might lay ahead."

They both leaned back in their seats and toasted to their respective futures, smiling at each other as they did so.

# Epilogue

Six months later, after discovering that she was pregnant with twins, Veronica Barron and Billy Bennett bought a big old Victorian house on Orchard Street in Dover, a little more than a mile from their old apartment on Baker Avenue. They were pleasantly surprised to learn that a couple of their neighbors were the brother and sister-in-law of Salvatore Bertoli...owner of Sallie's Bella Luna Tratoria, their favorite restaurant. Sallie's handsome nephew, Anthony, was one of the two young rambunctious boys always playing out and around in the neighborhood. Veronica laughed when she first heard that Anthony's best friend, Baxter, called him Ant.

Ten months later, having discarded his original working title of *Dressed To Kill*, Devon Stone's latest book, *Fatal Aria*, hit the best-seller lists in the U.K.

Confession must have been good for the soul, because Jian Hyui had been extremely forthright in his many conversations with Devon. Partially inspired by what Hyui had done in Kowloon Walled City, Devon remembered a line from a ballad sung in that opera about Mulan:

189

*"When a pair of rabbits run side by side, who can distinguish male from female?"* He therefore created a character, Renata Caballé, who was a beautiful and popular diva performing at the Royal Opera House in London. But she had a dark secret. *Very* dark. Late at night...*very* late... she would dress as a man luring and then savagely slaying prostitutes on the prowl, slashing their throats. Jack the Ripper redux. With a slight nod, perhaps, to Sweeney Todd, minus the meat pies, of course. A very dapper, intrepid police inspector was the one to finally solve the violent crimes, but not before being framed and accused of the crimes by the lying murderess.

Devon had made a solemn promise to Jian that he would never divulge to his sister, Lydia Hyui, his uncharacteristic and violent doings in that dark, foreboding place. And Jian promised to Devon that those doings have ceased. And were never to resume.

The following year *Heroines on Broomsticks*, a book written by Jeremy Fleck, won the prestigious Booker Prize, UK's top literary prize. A fictionalized telling of the soviet female pilots, the Night Witches, during World War II, Shepperton Studios soon thereafter bought the rights and turned it into a thrilling and successful film starring Anoushka Markarova. She portrayed the dramatized version of her own older sister, Aleksandra Markarova, who really *had been* one of the famous Night Witches.

Although it did not win, Peyton Chase escorted his wife, Anoushka Markarova, on the Red Carpet at the Academy Awards ceremony in Hollywood when her movie about the Night Witches was nominated for Best Foreign Film. With his strikingly handsome face, rugged body, and outgoing personality, he attracted the attention of a talent agent and was asked while conversing with him at a party later that evening if he would be interested in auditioning for a new, upcoming television series. The request, which had come as a total surprise and shock, took him aback. He graciously declined; laughing raucously about it with Billy Bennett over drinks one evening a few days later. Not a fan of westerns, he thought the premise sounded ludicrous. The show was *Have Gun — Will Travel*, and the lead role eventually went to a little-known actor at the time, Richard Boone.

Samuel Fleck *had*, indeed, written another book. Jeremy Fleck discovered the manuscript locked away in a safe deposit box in his father's bank while he was trying to settle the estate. It was not a thriller. It was not a roman à clef. It was an autobiography. It was blunt. It was brutally honest. It was profane. And it was potentially licentious in its dealings with Samuel's lies, deceptions and indiscretions throughout the years, including an infatuation of sorts with an opera singer performing with the Cantonese Opera Company in Hong Kong. More surprisingly, it was very well written.

Apparently dead men *do* tell tales.

Jeremy Fleck cried like a newborn baby when he read the extremely affectionate dedication, to him, with profound, heartfelt apologies and regrets for all the lost years of his father's love and respect for him.

Its publication is still pending.

# Author's Notes

*"Every murderer is probably somebody's old friend."*
Agatha Christie

My wife and I celebrated her 50th birthday while we were in Hong Kong. After spending nearly three weeks traveling throughout mainland China and eating nothing but Chinese food, albeit *real* Chinese food, on her birthday we dined very nicely at the best steak house in Hong Kong: Jimmy's Kitchen. A great way to celebrate, indeed! Although it may not have been, at the time we felt that we had just eaten the best roast prime rib of beef that we had ever had.

Hong Kong afforded us many pleasures, visual and culinary. The views from Victoria Peak were stunning. We enjoyed visiting local markets, including jewelry stores, and then having a stylish cashmere suit made (for me) and having a gorgeous silk dress made (for my wife). By the way, I can still wear that suit and it is still very much in style. Yet, the simplest and most enjoyable of our pleasures were our countless trips crossing Victoria Harbour back and forth from Kowloon Peninsula to Hong Kong Island on the Star Ferry. If I remember correctly, the fare at that time, in 1992, was the equivalent to 15¢.

The ride to the top of Victoria Peak was a thrilling experience on the historic old funicular, the Peak Tram.

A thrilling way to celebrate my wife's 50th birthday! We were very fortunate to have crystal clear skies. We roamed around on top of the peak enjoying every possible spectacular vista just as Devon Stone and Lydia Hyui do in this book.

With apologies to persnickety fact-checkers, I have taken a few liberties with the history of the Peninsula Hotel in Hong Kong and their renowned airport transfer service. They did not start that exclusive service with a fleet of Rolls-Royces until 1970. Each car, hand-made at the Rolls-Royce factory in Goodwood, England was finished in the signature Peninsula Green. The beautifully restored 1934 Phantom II that transported Devon Stone and Lydia Hyui was not actually purchased and introduced into this service until 1994.

The notorious, infamous, foreboding Kowloon Walled City actually existed. As quoted by Leung Ping-kwan in his writing "City of Darkness":

*Here, prostitutes installed themselves on one side of the street while a priest preached and handed out powdered milk to the poor on the other; social workers gave guidance while drug addicts squatted under the stairs getting high; what were children's games centers by day became strip-show venues by night. It was a very complex place, difficult to generalize about, a place that seemed frightening but where most people continued to lead normal lives. A place just like the rest of Hong Kong.*

In 1984, Britain and China began discussions regarding the problems of the notorious area, and subsequently announced the demolition of the City. Between 1987 and 1989 residents were resettled and demolition began in 1993. By 1995, the area had been transformed into a beautiful park designed as a Jiangnan garden of the early Qing dynasty. The award-winning park is divided into eight theme zones with their own characteristic scenery: Old South Gate, Eight Floral Walks, Garden of Four Seasons, Garden of Chinese Zodiac, Chess Garden, Mountain View Pavilion, Fei Sing Garden, and Guibi Rock. You might want to Google Kowloon Walled City Park for much more information and photographs. That once exceedingly dangerous enclave is now a tranquil place of beauty. Fascinating.

Another tidbit for all you history aficionado fact-checkers: Despite what Devon Stone told James Flynn, the capital of China, Peking, didn't become formally known as Beijing until 1979.

One final note that needs repeating: I mentioned in my Author's Notes in *Remember You Must Die* that there actually was a Broadway musical based upon *The Thin Man*. The musical was called, believe it or not, *Nick*

*& Nora*. It starred the handsome Barry Bostwick and the beautiful Joanna Gleason. It is *not* fondly remembered by anyone. It opened on December 8, 1991 and closed abruptly nine performances later. Brutally, ruthlessly shot through the heart by every New York City drama critic.

# Acknowledgements

*"No tears in the writer, no tears in the reader.*
*No surprise in the writer, no surprise in the reader."*
Robert Frost

I sincerely hope that I may have given *you*, the reader, a few surprises along the way. I surprised *myself* a few times while writing this book, and the story ended up a bit differently than I had originally intended. My characters developed minds of their own and led me in a couple diverse directions at times. That happens. Any shed tears may have depended upon your own attitudes and family histories. Not that I had expected you to keep count, but several father characters figured into the narrative throughout this book in one way or another.

Speaking of which, I never got to know my birth father, as he and my mother divorced when I was a toddler. That was back in the mid 1940s, *long* before the Internet, GOOGLE or Ancestry.com. My mother then remarried. My stepfather adopted me soon thereafter, thus changing my name. While he and I were never what I would call close, we understood each other despite our many social, political and philosophical differences. Actually we began to *really* appreciate and understand each other's views shortly before his sudden and unexpected death. That was a pity and I sincerely regret the time lost.

My birth father had also remarried and sired eight other children following *my* birth. On top of that, he had been married *before* marrying my mother and had two children with his first wife. They all knew that I existed somewhere. But where? I was a missing sibling until I was "discovered" by them when I was seventy years old. That unto itself could probably be another book. I would just have to try to figure out how to put a murder in it.

Via the wonders of the Internet and Ancestry.com, I thank the perseverance of my cousin Diane Berg Milioto and the curiosity of my daughter-in-law Tracy Hasbrouck for enabling me to unite with a family I never even knew existed.

While my birth father never pursued art as a career, I recently learned that he liked to draw. Hence, the excellent pencil sketch self-portrait as illustrated here. The irony here is that I had loved to draw from an extremely young age, winning art contests throughout the years, and actually had a long, successful, award-winning career as a graphic designer.

Ladislaw Fried, Self-Portrait

As in the Acknowledgements of my previous five books, I thank my two amazing sons, Gregory and Christopher, for putting up with me throughout the years. I truly hope we have not had *too* many "Daddy Issues" but then I can be oblivious at times. And, again, I can only assume that neither one plotted my demise.

I give a warm and loving nod to two of my handsome grandsons, Devon Stone Hasbrouck and Peyton Chase Hasbrouck, for allowing me to use their first and middle names for two of my favorite characters.

I thank my faithful readers (hopefully a growing number) for giving me continued encouragement. They claim to want me to keep writing my feeble attempts at fiction, thrillers or otherwise. Neither Ernest Hemingway nor Mark Greaney have anything to fear. The book clubs that have invited me to appear and speak have stroked my ego beyond repair. I shall be forever grateful.

But the largest chunk of platinum-quality gratitude goes to my very best friend, my wife of fifty-nine years, Gaylin, who has been patient *way* beyond words. I promised her that *Horse Scents* would be my one and only book having usurping many hours (months) of my time. But then along came *Stable Affairs*…and *Down With The Sun*, followed by *Murder On The Street Of Years*, *Remember You Must Die*, and eventually I came up with *Another Word For Murder*. A promise made and promises broken. I drive that poor woman bats!

Printed in the United States
by Baker & Taylor Publisher Services